Mm Nn Oo Pp

Mm Nn Oo Pp

Qq Rr Ss Tt

Qq Rr Ss Tt

Uu Vv Ww Xx

Uu Vv Ww Xx

Yy Zz

Yy Zz

除
還

NEW全彩學生快速記憶

英語圖鑑字典

情境學習常用單字、片語和會話句型
Best English Picture Dictionary for Students

監修 佐藤久美子（日本玉川大學研究所名譽教授．特任教授）
審訂 馮和平（臺灣師範大學英語學系副教授）

附雙CD

給使用這本書的讀者

　　我希望大家能以閱讀繪本或漫畫的感覺，愉悅的閱讀這本《NEW全彩學生快速記憶英語圖鑑字典》，並從中學會各種常用單字。這本《NEW全彩學生快速記憶英語圖鑑字典》包含大約2300個單字、片語和會話句型。當你思考著「自然科學教室」的英語怎麼說？「運動會」的英語是什麼？就趕快翻開這本書吧！如果記住2000個以上的單字，你就能成為英語會話高手。經常將這本書放在身旁，究竟會記住多少單字呢？真令人期待！

　　想一想，如果你能說英語，會發生什麼快樂的事？當你去國外，可以憑藉自己的能力向店員購買漢堡或薯條，會有多自豪、多開心！若還因此交到外國朋友，也會很高興吧！先從用英語自我介紹開始試試看！

My name is Anna.（我的名字是安娜。）

I'm ten years old.（我十歲。）

I live in Tokyo.（我住在東京。）

接下來問朋友。

Do you have any pets？（你有養什麼寵物嗎？）

　　這本書中，有許多像這樣的對話。你可以找家人或朋友練習，成為一個英語會話高手吧！

讓孩子從小接觸英語，能擴展他們的興趣和世界觀！

孩子擁有適應異國文化和不同環境的能力，只要讓孩子從小接觸並習慣使用英語，他們的興趣也會增加。若將這本《NEW全彩學生快速記憶英語圖鑑字典》作為英語學習教材，孩子能從中發覺母語和英語的不同，並感受到文化之間的差異，產生無比的好奇心。

這本書中包含迷宮和找一找等遊戲設計，並搭配能讓孩子會心一笑的插圖，讓孩子自然而然對學英語產生興趣，萌生自主學習的動力。此外，這本書還附有CD，孩子可以聽一聽單字及片語的發音，培養語彙能力及會話能力。

若家長和老師手邊有這本書，除了能立即回答孩子的疑問，也能當成日常英語讀物哦！

活用此書的方式

連結文字與情境來加深印象

要自然的學會一種語言，就要讓孩子將情境和詞句連結在一起，藉此加深印象。這本書將情境以插圖的方式呈現，只要配合插圖一起熟記單字，在遇到相同情境時，就能自然的開口說英語。

反覆練習單字及片語

不斷重複的話語才能留下深刻的印象。因此請務必善加運用CD，藉由一邊聽，一邊朗讀的過程，增加記得的單字及片語數量。

學習英語，是為了培育孩子的溝通能力，讓孩子在他人面前能充滿自信的說出想法和意見。我衷心希望透過本書學英語的孩子，都能擁有寬廣宏大的世界觀。

—— 佐藤久美子（日本玉川大學研究所名譽教授・特任教授）

本書使用方法

CD的曲目編號

附有CD的曲目編號。請搭配曲目編號來聆聽CD。每一跨頁的音檔收錄在同一個曲目編號中。CD分成CD1和CD2。

會話句型

依照情境設定會話句型。全都是對日常生活及上課有幫助的詞句,請試著念出來。

CD朗讀順序編號

CD會從編號❶的單字開始依序朗讀。

音標

全部的單字都有標注音標。雖然音標的拼音極為接近實際的發音,但學習英語的發音還是要以CD的發音為準。

英語單字的中文意思

這本書收錄大約 2300 個生活常用單字、片語及會話句型，並依照情境分類，亦都標示了中文意思。本書的英語單字主要是以原形、單數型態來呈現，不過，在會話中大多以複數型態表示的單字，則以複數表示。此外，有關美國與英國用法不同的單字，將以美國的用法為主。

⑥ school festival
[ˋskul] [ˋfɛstəvl]
校慶

⑦ spring vacation
[ˋsprɪŋ] [veˋkeʃən]
春假

⑧ summer vacation
[ˋsʌmə] [veˋkeʃən]
暑假

⑨ winter vacation
[ˋwɪntə] [veˋkeʃən]
寒假

⑩ graduation
[͵grædʒuˋeʃən]
畢業、
畢業典禮

各國新學期的開學日和暑假長度不太一樣，例如：臺灣通常在 8 月底或 9 月初展開新學期，暑假大約兩個月；日本則是在 4 月展開新學期，暑假一個多月左右。

163

精采插圖

書中運用豐富的插圖表現各種生活情境。可以一邊看著可愛的插圖，一邊快樂的學習各種事物該如何用英語表達。

專欄

介紹臺灣與美國、英國等國家的文化差異，還有使用英語時該注意的地方。

第 226～254 頁為索引。如果想查詢某個單字卻不知道在哪一頁時，就來翻閱索引吧！

CONTENTS 目次

PERSON… 人

HOUSE… 家

FOOD… 食物

TOWN… 城鎮

SCHOOL … 學校

NATURE … 大自然

SPORTS and AMUSEMENTS … 運動和娛樂

EVENTS … 事件

CONTENTS　目次

LIFE··· 生活

COLORS, SHAPES and NUMBERS··· 顏色、形狀和數字

ENGLISH··· 英語

8

PERSON

[ˋpɝsn̩]

Let's Introduce Ourselves
[lɛts] [ˌɪntrəˈdjus] [ˌaʊrˈsɛlvz]

來自我介紹吧！

CD1
03

88頁 **School** 學校

I go to Kita Elementary School.
我就讀奇塔小學。

I will introduce myself.
我來自我介紹。

My name is Anna.
我的名字是安娜。

I'm in the fifth grade.
我五年級。

I'm ten years old.
我十歲。

190~193頁
Numbers
數字

I live in Tokyo.
我住在東京。

10

Questions to Your Friend
[ˈkwɛstʃənz] [tu] [jʊɚ] [frɛnd]

問一問你的朋友

CD1 04

What subject do you like?
你喜歡什麼科目？

I like P.E.
我喜歡體育課。

90 頁

School Subjects
學習科目

Do you have any pets?
你有養什麼寵物嗎？

Yes, I have a dog.
有，我養一隻狗。

What fruit do you like best?
你最喜歡什麼水果？

I like bananas.
我喜歡香蕉。

50 頁

Fruit
水果

104~109 頁 **Animals**
動物

What color do you like?
你喜歡什麼顏色？

I like blue.
我喜歡藍色。

186 頁 **Colors**
顏色

What time do you get up?
你什麼時候起床？

198 頁 **Time**
時間

At seven.
七點鐘。

12

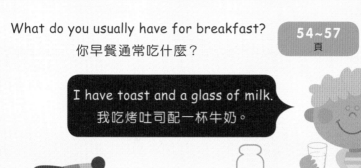

What do you usually have for breakfast?
你早餐通常吃什麼？

54~57
頁

Meals
餐點

I have toast and a glass of milk.
我吃烤吐司配一杯牛奶。

Milk

How do you go to school?
你怎麼去學校？

By bus.
搭公車。

80
頁

Transportation
交通工具

What sport do you like?
你喜歡什麼運動？

150~153
頁

Sports
運動

I like basketball.
我喜歡籃球。

When is your birthday?
你的生日是什麼時候？

156
頁

Months
月

It's December 2nd.
是12月2日。

Body

[ˈbɑdɪ]

身體

CD1 05

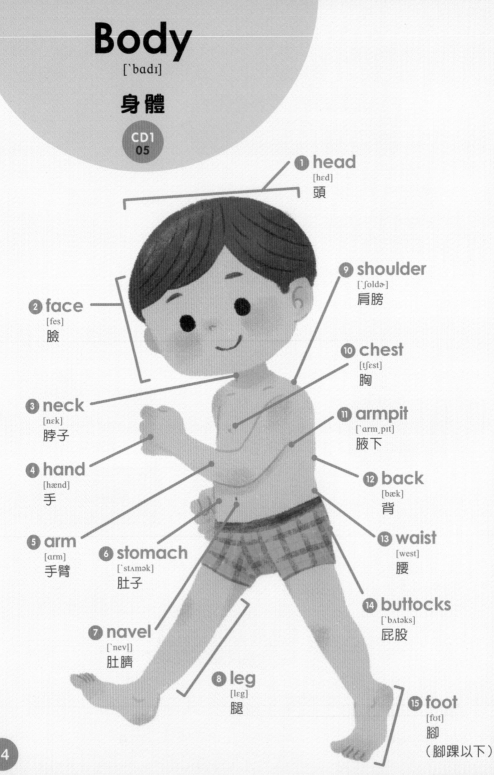

❶ head
[hɛd]
頭

❷ face
[fes]
臉

❸ neck
[nɛk]
脖子

❹ hand
[hænd]
手

❺ arm
[ɑrm]
手臂

❻ stomach
[ˈstʌmək]
肚子

❼ navel
[ˈnevl̩]
肚臍

❽ leg
[lɛg]
腿

❾ shoulder
[ˈʃoldɚ]
肩膀

❿ chest
[tʃɛst]
胸

⓫ armpit
[ˈɑrmˌpɪt]
腋下

⓬ back
[bæk]
背

⓭ waist
[west]
腰

⓮ buttocks
[ˈbʌtəks]
屁股

⓯ foot
[fʊt]
腳
（腳踝以下）

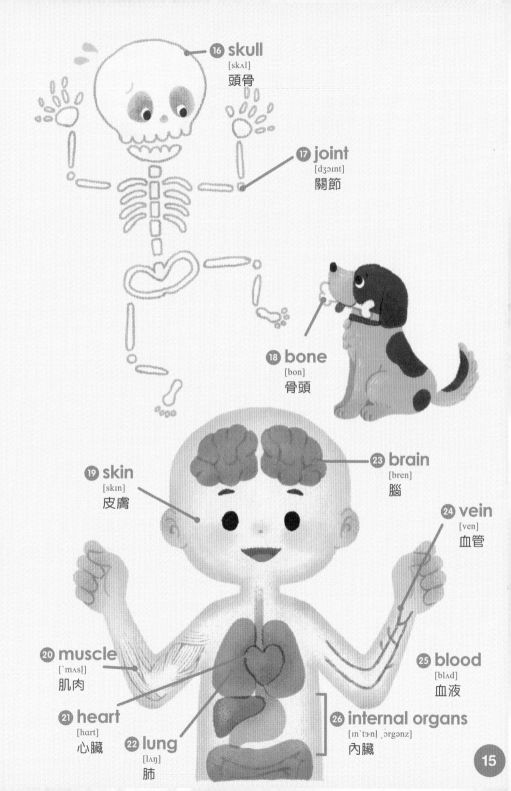

16 skull
[skʌl]
頭骨

17 joint
[dʒɔɪnt]
關節

18 bone
[bon]
骨頭

19 skin
[skɪn]
皮膚

23 brain
[bren]
腦

24 vein
[ven]
血管

20 muscle
[ˋmʌsl]
肌肉

21 heart
[hɑrt]
心臟

22 lung
[lʌŋ]
肺

25 blood
[blʌd]
血液

26 internal organs
[ɪnˋtɚnl ˏɔrgənz]
內臟

Feet

[fit]

腳

CD1 06

1 thigh
[θaɪ]
大腿

2 knee
[ni]
膝蓋

3 shin
[ʃɪn]
脛

4 calf
[kæf]
小腿肚

5 leg
[lɛg]
腿

7 toenail
[`to͵nel]
腳指甲

8 toe
[to]
腳趾

6 instep
[`ɪn͵stɛp]
腳背

9 ankle
[`æŋkl̩]
腳踝

10 foot
[fʊt]
腳（單數）

11 feet
[fit]
腳（複數）

12 heel
[hil]
腳後跟

13 sole
[sol]
腳底

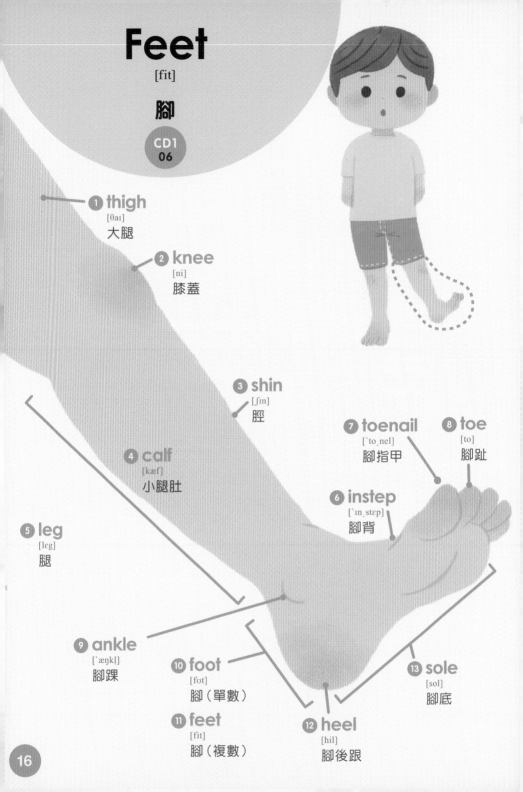

14 stand
[stænd]
站立

15 walk
[wɔk]
走

16 run
[rʌn]
跑

17 skip
[skɪp]
輕快的跳

18 jump
[dʒʌmp]
跳

19 hop
[hap]
單腳跳

20 sit
[sɪt]
坐

21 kick
[kɪk]
踢

22 stand up
[ˌstænd ˋʌp]
起立

23 slip
[slɪp]
滑

24 crawl
[krɔl]
爬

25 climb
[klaɪm]
攀爬

Hands

[hændz]

手

CD1 07

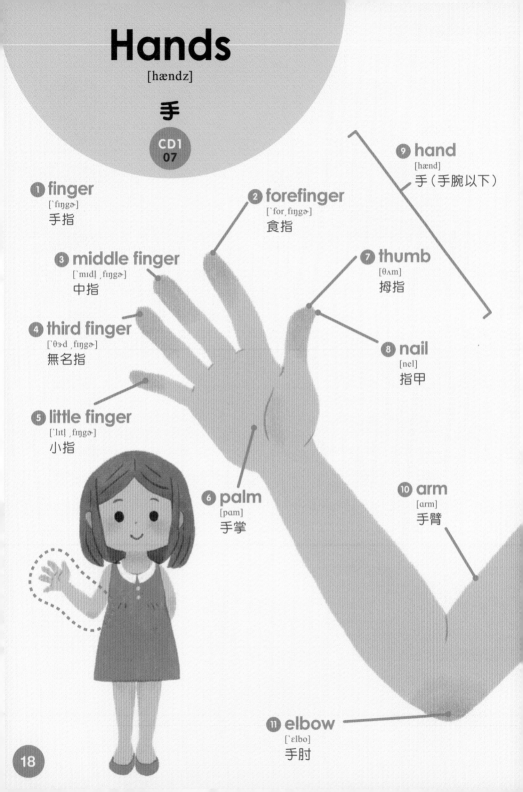

❶ finger
[ˋfɪŋgɚ]
手指

❷ forefinger
[ˋforˏfɪŋgɚ]
食指

❸ middle finger
[ˋmɪdl̩ˏfɪŋgɚ]
中指

❹ third finger
[ˋθɝd ˏfɪŋgɚ]
無名指

❺ little finger
[ˋlɪtl̩ ˏfɪŋgɚ]
小指

❻ palm
[pɑm]
手掌

❼ thumb
[θʌm]
拇指

❽ nail
[nel]
指甲

❾ hand
[hænd]
手（手腕以下）

❿ arm
[ɑrm]
手臂

⓫ elbow
[ˋɛlbo]
手肘

手部相關動作

 ⑫ **touch** 摸
[tʌtʃ]

 ⑬ **hold** 握
[hold]

 ⑭ **point** 指
[pɔɪnt]

 ⑮ **wave** 揮
[wev]

 ⑯ **grab** 抓
[græb]

 ⑰ **catch** 接
[kætʃ]

 ⑱ **throw** 投、擲、拋
[θro]

 ⑲ **press** 按
[prɛs]

 ⑳ **clap** 拍
[klæp]

 ㉑ **knock** 敲
[nɑk]

 ㉒ **scratch** 抓、劃
[skrætʃ]

 ㉓ **rub** 擦
[rʌb]

Face

[fes]

臉

CD1 08

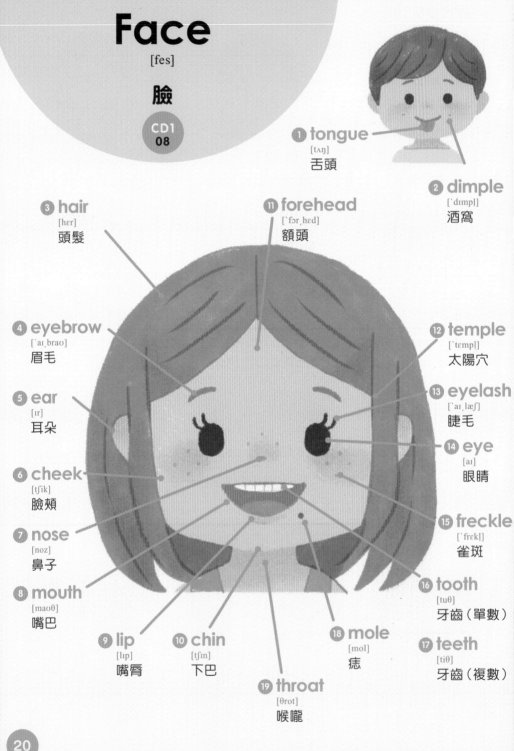

1 tongue
[tʌŋ]
舌頭

2 dimple
[ˋdɪmpl]
酒窩

3 hair
[hɛr]
頭髮

11 forehead
[ˋfɔr͵hɛd]
額頭

4 eyebrow
[ˋaɪ͵braʊ]
眉毛

5 ear
[ɪr]
耳朵

6 cheek
[tʃik]
臉頰

7 nose
[noz]
鼻子

8 mouth
[maʊθ]
嘴巴

9 lip
[lɪp]
嘴脣

10 chin
[tʃɪn]
下巴

12 temple
[ˋtɛmpl]
太陽穴

13 eyelash
[ˋaɪ͵læʃ]
睫毛

14 eye
[aɪ]
眼睛

15 freckle
[ˋfrɛkl]
雀斑

16 tooth
[tuθ]
牙齒（單數）

17 teeth
[tiθ]
牙齒（複數）

18 mole
[mol]
痣

19 throat
[θrot]
喉嚨

臉部相關動作

⑳ **watch** （觀）看
[watʃ]

㉑ **look at** （注意）看
[lʊk] [æt]

㉒ **see** （自然）看見
[si]

㉓ **hear** 聽
[hɪr]

㉔ **listen to** （注意）聽
[ˋlɪsn̩] [tu]

㉕ **smell** 聞
[smɛl]

㉖ **kiss** 親
[kɪs]

㉗ **whistle** 吹口哨
[ˋhwɪsl̩]

㉘ **smile** 微笑
[smaɪl]

㉙ **laugh** 大笑（笑出聲音）
[læf]

㉚ **cry** 哭（哭出聲音）
[kraɪ]

㉛ **weep** 流淚
[wip]

Personalities

[ˌpɝsn̩ˈælətɪz]

個性

CD1 09

3 polite
[pəˈlaɪt]
有禮貌的

2 cheerful
[ˈtʃɪrfəl]
高興的

1 humorous
[ˈhjumərəs]
幽默的

> **George is funny.**
> 喬治是個有趣的人。

5 friendly
[ˈfrɛndlɪ]
友善的

4 smart
[smɑrt]
聰明的

6 shy
[ʃaɪ]
害羞的

7 brave
[brev]
勇敢的

8 careful
[ˈkɛrfəl]
仔細的、
小心的

10 strict
[strɪkt]
嚴格的

11 honest
[ɑnɪst]
正直的

9 strong
[strɔŋ]
強壯的

12 kind
[kaɪnd]
親切的

13 patient
[`peʃənt]
能忍受的、
有耐心的

Tom is kind.
湯姆是個親切的人。

14 active
[`æktɪv]
活潑的

15 curious
[`kjʊrɪəs]
好奇的

23

Emotions
[ɪˈmoʃənz]

情緒

CD1
10

1 happy
[ˈhæpɪ]
快樂的

2 disappointed
[ˌdɪsəˈpɔɪntɪd]
沮喪的

3 sad
[sæd]
悲傷的

4 lonely
[ˈlonlɪ]
孤單的

5 bored
[bord]
無聊的

6 surprised
[səˈpraɪzd]
驚訝的

7 worried
[ˈwɝɪd]
煩惱的

8 moved
[muvd]
感動的

9 shocked
[ʃɑkt]
震驚的

How do you feel now?
你現在感覺如何？

I'm happy.
我覺得很快樂。

⑩ delighted
[dɪˋlaɪtɪd]
高興的

⑪ angry
[ˋæŋgrɪ]
生氣的

⑫ satisfied
[ˋsætɪsˏfaɪd]
滿足的

⑬ amused
[əˋmjuzd]
被逗樂的

⑭ afraid
[əˋfred]
害怕的

⑮ anxious
[ˋæŋkʃəs]
焦慮的

⑯ nervous
[ˋnɝvəs]
緊張的

⑰ annoyed
[əˋnɔɪd]
惱怒的

⑱ confused
[kənˋfjuzd]
困惑的

25

Family

[ˋfæməlɪ]

家庭

CD1
11

❶ grandparents
[ˋgrænd͵pɛrənts]
外祖父母

❷ grandmother
[ˋgrænd͵mʌðɚ]
外祖母／外婆

❸ grandfather
[ˋgrænd͵fɑðɚ]
外祖父／外公

❻ parents
[ˋpɛrənts]
父母

❹ uncle
[ˋʌŋkl̩]
姨丈

❺ aunt
[ænt]
阿姨

❼ mother
[ˋmʌðɚ]
媽媽

❽ father
[ˋfɑðɚ]
爸爸

❾ cousin
[ˋkʌzn̩]
表兄弟姊妹

❿ sister
[ˋsɪstɚ]
姊姊／妹妹

⓫ I / me
[aɪ]／[mi]
我

⓬ brother
[ˋbrʌðɚ]
哥哥／弟弟

This is a photo of my family.

這是我的全家福照片。

You have two older brothers.

你有兩個哥哥。

grandparents
[`grænd,perənts]
祖父母

grandmother
[`grænd,mʌðə]
祖母／奶奶

grandfather
[`grænd,faðə]
祖父／爺爺

uncle
[`ʌŋkl]
伯父／
叔叔

aunt
[ænt]
伯母／
嬸嬸

cousin
[`kʌzn]
堂兄弟姊妹

 如果想多描述你的兄弟姊妹，可以用 older brother 表示哥哥、younger brother 表示弟弟、older sister 表示姊姊、younger sister 表示妹妹。另外，uncle 還包含舅舅、姑丈的意思；aunt 還包含舅媽、姑姑的意思。

與家族相關的單字

CD1
12

介紹家人、親屬稱謂相關單字。

1 child
[tʃaɪld]
孩子（單數）

2 children
[`tʃɪldrən]
孩子（複數）

3 son
[sʌn]
兒子

4 daughter
[`dɔtɚ]
女兒

5 baby
[`bebɪ]
嬰兒

6 niece
[nis]
外甥女、姪女

7 nephew
[`nɛfju]
外甥、姪兒

8 grandchild
[`grænd͵tʃaɪld]
孫子、孫女

9 husband
[`hʌzbənd]
丈夫

10 wife
[waɪf]
妻子

11 second cousin
[`sɛkənd] [`kʌzn̩]
父母的堂（或表）兄弟
姊妹的子女

12 relative
[`rɛlətɪv]
親戚

HOUSE

[haʊs]

家

Around the House
[əˈraʊnd] [ðə] [haʊs]

住家周遭

CD1 13

6 ceilin
[ˈsilɪŋ]
天花板

7 ha
[hɔl]
門廳

1 second floor
[ˈsɛkənd] [flor]
二樓

2 first floor
[fɝst] [flor]
一樓

5 study
[ˈstʌdɪ]
書房

3 garage
[gəˈrɑʒ]
車庫

14 stairs
[stɛrz]
樓梯

15 floor
[flor]
地板

Welcome to my house.
歡迎來我家。

4 dining room
[ˈdaɪnɪŋ ˌrum]
飯廳

Thank you for inviting me.
謝謝你邀請我。

10 attic
[ˈætɪk]
閣樓

11 chimney
[ˈtʃɪmnɪ]
煙囪

9 roof
[ruf]
屋頂

8 wall
[wɔl]
牆壁

13 window
[ˈwɪndo]
窗戶

12 bedroom
[ˈbɛdˌrʊm]
臥房

22 neighbor
[ˈnebɚ]
鄰居

16 living room
[ˈlɪvɪŋ ˌrʊm]
客廳

17 bathroom
[ˈbæθˌrʊm]
浴室

18 front door
[frʌnt] [dor]
正門

19 mailbox
[ˈmelˌbɑks]

20 yard
[jɑrd]
庭院

21 fence
[fɛns]
圍籬

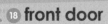

英式英語將一樓稱作 ground floor，二樓稱作
first floor。

31

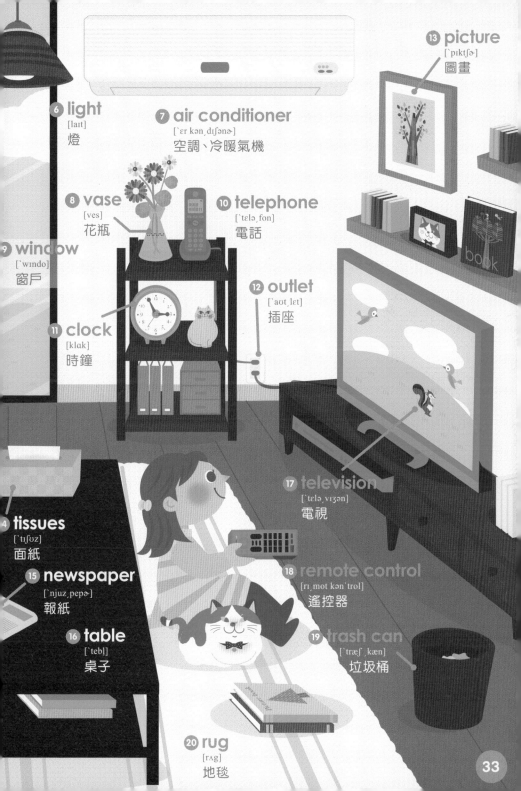

6 light
[laɪt]
燈

7 air conditioner
[`ɛr kənˌdɪʃənɚ]
空調、冷暖氣機

13 picture
[`pɪktʃɚ]
圖畫

8 vase
[ves]
花瓶

10 telephone
[`tɛləˌfon]
電話

9 window
[`wɪndo]
窗戶

12 outlet
[`aʊtˌlɛt]
插座

11 clock
[klɑk]
時鐘

17 television
[`tɛləˌvɪʒən]
電視

4 tissues
[`tɪʃʊz]
面紙

15 newspaper
[`njuzˌpepɚ]
報紙

18 remote control
[rɪ`mot kən`trol]
遙控器

16 table
[`tebl̩]
桌子

19 trash can
[`træʃˌkæn]
垃圾桶

20 rug
[rʌg]
地毯

33

In the Dining Room

[ɪn] [ðə] [ˈdaɪnɪŋ ˌrum]

在飯廳裡

CD1
15

❷ pepper shaker
[ˈpɛpɚ ˌʃekɚ]
胡椒罐

❶ salt shaker
[ˈsɔlt ˌʃekɚ]
鹽罐

> **Please set the table.**
> 請擺好餐具。

❽ table
[ˈtebl̩]
桌子

❾ napkin
[ˈnæpkɪn]
餐巾

⓯ chair
[tʃɛr]
椅子

34

③ cup
[kʌp]
杯子

④ plate
[plet]
盤子

⑤ cupboard
[ˋkʌbəd]
櫥櫃

⑥ glass
[glæs]
玻璃杯

⑦ bottle opener
[ˋbɑtl ˋopənə]
開瓶器

OK.
好的。

⑩ chopsticks
[ˋtʃɑpˌstɪks]
筷子

⑪ bowl
[bol]
碗

⑫ fork
[fɔrk]
叉子

⑬ knife
[naɪf]
刀子

⑭ spoon
[spun]
湯匙

⑯ tablecloth
[ˋteblˌklɔθ]
桌巾

BEER

In the Kitchen

[ɪn] [ðə] [ˈkɪtʃɪn]

在廚房裡

CD1 16

1 kitchen fan
[ˈkɪtʃɪn ˌfæn]
抽油煙機

6 whisk
[hwɪsk]
攪拌器

5 ladle
[ˈledl]
杓子

2 refrigerator
[rɪˈfrɪdʒəˌretɚ]
冰箱

4 frying pan
[ˈfraɪŋ ˌpæn]
煎鍋

8 pot
[pɑt]
鍋子

9 lid
[lɪd]
蓋子

3 freezer
[ˈfrizɚ]
冷凍庫

7 stove
[stov]
爐子

15 oven
[ˈʌvən]
烤箱

What's for dinner?

晚餐吃什麼？

19 rice cooker
[ˈraɪs ˌkʊkɚ]
電鍋

⑩ kettle
[ˋkɛtl]
壺

Steak and salad.
牛排和沙拉。

⑪ cutting board
[ˋkʌtɪŋ ˌbord]
砧板

⑫ kitchen knife
[ˋkɪtʃɪn ˌnaɪf]
菜刀

⑬ sink
[sɪŋk]
水槽

⑭ dish towel
[ˋdɪʃ ˌtaʊəl]
擦碗布

⑯ dishwasher
[ˋdɪʃ ˌwɑʃɚ]
洗碗機

⑰ apron
[ˋeprən]
圍裙

⑱ microwave oven
[ˋmaɪkro wev ˋʌvən]
微波爐

⑳ bowl
[bol]
碗

㉒ measuring spoon
[ˋmɛʒrɪŋ ˌspun]
量匙

㉑ measuring cup
[ˋmɛʒrɪŋ ˌkʌp]
量杯

㉓ peeler
[ˋpilɚ]
削皮器

37

In the Bedroom
[ɪn] [ðə] [`bɛd͵rʊm]

在臥房裡

CD1
17

3 dresser
[`drɛsɚ]
梳妝臺

4 shelf
[ʃɛlf]
架子

1 alarm clock
[ə`lɑrm ͵klɑk]
鬧鐘

2 lamp
[læmp]
燈

Good night, Dad.

晚安，爸爸。

7 pillow
[`pɪlo]
枕頭

10 blanket
[`blæŋkɪt]
毯子

11 comforter
[`kʌmfɚtɚ]
棉被

8 sheet
[ʃit]
床單

9 mattress
[`mætrɪs]
床墊

14 sleep
[slip]
睡覺

15 yawn
[jɔn]
打呵欠

16 dream
[drim]
做夢

17 wake up
[͵wek `ʌp]
起床

38

6 closet
['klɑzɪt]
衣櫃

5 drawer
['drɔɚ]
抽屜

12 bed
[bɛd]
床

> Sleep tight, Rina. Sweet dreams.
> 睡個好覺，蕾娜。祝你有個好夢。

13 desk
[dɛsk]
書桌

18 go to bed
[go] [tu] [bɛd]
就寢

19 take a nap
[tek] [ə] [næp]
打盹

20 oversleep
[ˌovɚ'slip]
睡過頭

39

In the Bathroom 1
[ɪn] [ðə] [`bæθˌrum] [wʌn]

在浴室裡1

CD1
18

1 **mirror**
[`mɪrɚ]
鏡子

2 **hand towel**
[`hænd ˌtaʊəl]
擦手巾

3 **faucet**
[`fɔsɪt]
水龍頭

5 **hand soap**
[`hænd ˌsop]
洗手乳

7 **sink**
[sɪŋk]
水槽

4 **cabinet**
[`kæbənɪt]
櫃子

6 **scale**
[skel]
體重計

8 **bath mat**
[`bæθ ˌmæt]
浴室地墊

toothbrush
[ˈtuθ͵brʌʃ]
牙刷

10 toothpaste
[ˈtuθ͵pest]
牙膏

11 hairbrush
[ˈhɛr͵brʌʃ]
梳子

12 hairdryer
[ˈhɛr͵draɪɚ]
吹風機

13 weigh myself
[we] [maɪˈsɛlf]
量體重

14 wash my face
[wɑʃ] [maɪ] [fes]
洗臉

15 wash my hands
[wɑʃ] [maɪ] [hændz]
洗手

16 gargle
[ˈgargl̩]
漱喉、漱口

17 brush my teeth
[brʌʃ] [maɪ] [tiθ]
刷牙

18 rinse my mouth
[rɪns] [maɪ] [mauθ]
漱口

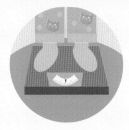

19 brush my hair
[brʌʃ] [maɪ] [hɛr]
梳頭髮

20 dry my hair
[draɪ] [maɪ] [hɛr]
吹頭髮

In the Bathroom 2

[ɪn] [ðə] [ˋbæθˌrum] [tu]

在浴室裡2

CD1 19

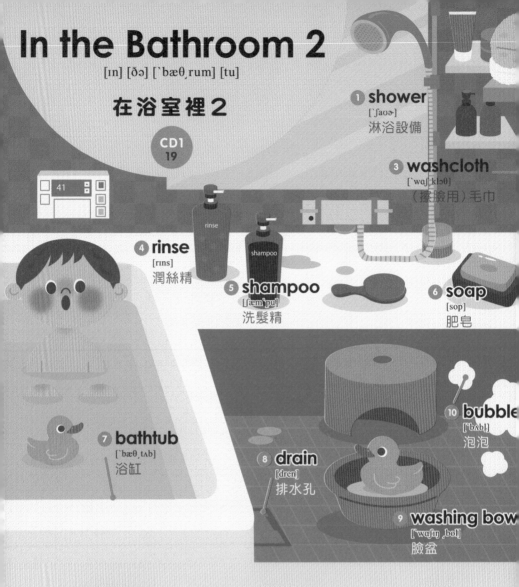

1 shower
[ˋʃaʊɚ]
淋浴設備

3 washcloth
[ˋwaʃˌklɔθ]
（擦臉用）毛巾

4 rinse
[rɪns]
潤絲精

5 shampoo
[ʃæmˋpu]
洗髮精

6 soap
[sop]
肥皂

7 bathtub
[ˋbæθˌtʌb]
浴缸

8 drain
[dren]
排水孔

10 bubble
[ˋbʌbl]
泡泡

9 washing bowl
[ˋwaʃɪŋ ˌbol]
臉盆

13 wash myself
[waʃ] [maɪˋsɛlf]
洗澡

14 wash my hair
[waʃ] [maɪ] [hɛr]
洗頭

15 take a shower
[tek] [ə] [ˋʃaʊɚ]
淋浴

42

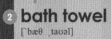

② bath towel
[ˋbæθ ˏtaʊəl]
浴巾

May I use the bathroom?

我可以使用浴室嗎?

⑪ toilet paper
[ˋtɔɪlɪt ˏpepɚ]
衛生紙

Sure.

當然。

⑫ toilet
[ˋtɔɪlɪt]
馬桶

⑯ flush the toilet
[flʌʃ] [ðə] [ˋtɔɪlɪt]
沖馬桶

⑰ go to the bathroom
[go] [tu] [ðə] [ˋbæθ ˏrum]
去洗手間

In the Yard

[ɪn] [ðə] [jɑrd]

在庭院裡

CD1
20

6 shovel
[`ʃʌvl]
鏟子

7 hose
[hoz]
水管

1 hedge
[hɛdʒ]
樹籬

I'll water the flowers

我來澆花。

2 flowerbed
[`flauə‚bɛd]
花圃

8 fertilizer
[`fɝtə‚laɪzə]
肥料

3 watering can
[`wɔtərɪŋ ‚kæn]
灑水壺

9 lawn
[lɔn]
草坪

4 soil
[sɔɪl]
泥土

5 brick
[brɪk]
磚塊

10 bucket
[`bʌkɪt]
水桶

44

11 tree
[tri]
樹

13 hammock
[ˋhæmək]
吊床

12 flowerpot
[ˋflaʊɚˌpɑt]
花盆

I'll weed the garden then.

那麼，我來除草。

14 doghouse
[ˋdɔgˌhaʊs]
狗屋

DOG

yard是指住家周邊的庭園。garden是yard的一部分，
是用來種植與維護花草樹木的地方。

Housework

[`haʊsˌwɜ·k]

家事

1 dryer
[`draɪə]
烘乾機

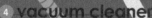

CD1 21

Thanks, Nobu.

謝謝，諾布。

3 dustpan
[`dʌstˌpæn]
畚箕

2 washing machine
[`wɑʃɪŋ məˌʃin]
洗衣機

4 vacuum cleaner
[`vækjʊəm ˌklinə]
吸塵器

5 broom
[brum]
掃帚

6 dust
[dʌst]
灰塵

Mom, I can help you.

媽媽，我可以幫你。

7 dish
[dɪʃ]
碟子、盤子

8 dish towel
[`dɪʃ ˌtaʊəl]
擦碗布

46

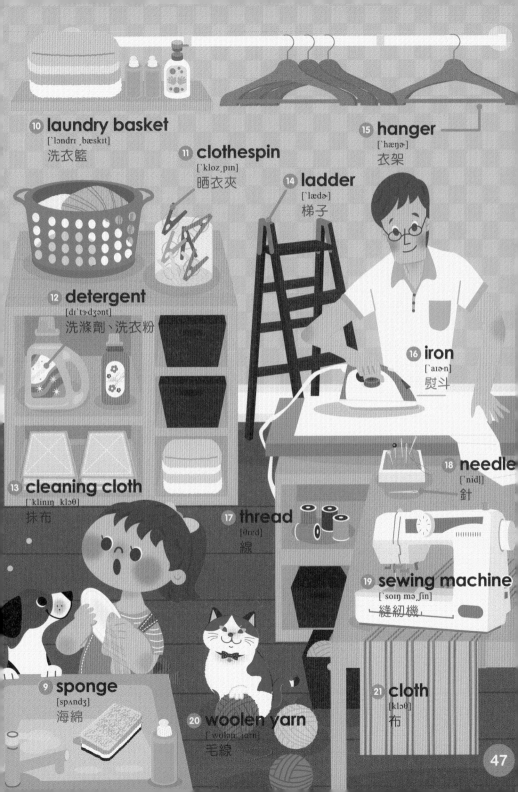

10 laundry basket
[`lɔndrɪ ˌbæskɪt]
洗衣籃

11 clothespin
[`kloz͵pɪn]
晒衣夾

14 ladder
[`lædə]
梯子

15 hanger
[`hæŋə]
衣架

12 detergent
[dɪ`tɝdʒənt]
洗滌劑、洗衣粉

16 iron
[`aɪə-n]
熨斗

13 cleaning cloth
[`klinɪŋ ͵klɔθ]
抹布

18 needle
[`nidl]
針

17 thread
[θrɛd]
線

19 sewing machine
[`soɪŋ mə͵ʃin]
縫紉機

9 sponge
[spʌndʒ]
海綿

20 woolen yarn
[`wʊlən ͵jarn]
毛線

21 cloth
[klɔθ]
布

47

與家事相關的單字

CD1 22

可以用這些單字來描述做家事。

❶ clean
[klin]
清潔

❷ cook
[kʊk]
煮

❸ wash
[wɑʃ]
洗

❹ wipe
[waɪp]
擦拭

❺ sweep
[swip]
清掃

❻ sew
[so]
縫紉

❼ knit
[nɪt]
編織

❽ bundle
[ˋbʌndl]
綑綁

❾ squeeze
[skwiz]
擰、壓

❿ water the flowers
[ˋwɔtɚ] [ðə] [ˋflaʊɚz]
澆花

⓫ weed
[wid]
除草

⓬ mow
[mo]
割草

FOOD

[fud]

食物

Fruit
[frut]

水果

CD1
23

〈和水果相關的單字〉

❶ rind
[raɪnd]
（硬的）果皮

❷ flesh
[flɛʃ]
果肉

❸ seed 種子
[sid]

❹ peel
[pil]
果皮

❺ shell
[ʃɛl]
果殼

❻ banana
[bə`nænə]
香蕉

❼ pineapple
[`paɪnˏæpl]
鳳梨

❽ coconut
[`kokənət]
椰子

❾ pear
[pɛr]
梨

❿ papaya
[pə`paɪə]
木瓜

⓫ blueberry
[`bluˏbɛrɪ]
藍莓

⓬ fig
[fɪg]
無花果

⓭ avocado
[ˏɑvə`kado]
酪梨

⓮ kiwi (fruit)
[`kiwɪ (frut)]
奇異果

⓯ tangerine
[ˏtændʒə`rin]
橘子、紅橘

⓰ orange
[`ɔrɪndʒ]
柳橙、柑橘

⓱ grapefruit
[`grepˏfrut]
葡萄柚

50

What's your favorite fruit?
你最喜歡什麼水果？

Strawberries.
草莓。

19 melon
[ˋmɛlən]
哈密瓜

20 strawberry
[ˋstrɔˌbɛrɪ]
草莓

18 apple
[ˋæpl̩]
蘋果

21 lemon
[ˋlɛmən]
檸檬

22 mango
[ˋmæŋgo]
芒果

23 persimmon
[pəˋsɪmən]
柿子

24 cherry
[ˋtʃɛrɪ]
櫻桃

25 peach
[pitʃ]
水蜜桃

28 walnut
[ˋwɔlnət]
核桃

26 grapes
[greps]
葡萄

27 Japanese pear
[ˋdʒæpənɪz ˌpɛr]
白梨

29 chestnut
[ˋtʃɛsˌnʌt]
栗子

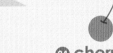

Vegetables
[ˈvɛdʒətəblz]

蔬菜

CD1
24

1 turnip
[ˈtɝnɪp]
蕪菁

4 lettuce
[ˈlɛtəs]
萵苣

5 cabbage
[ˈkæbɪdʒ]
甘藍

6 onion
[ˈʌnjən]
洋蔥

2 parsley
[ˈparslɪ]
香芹

7 broccoli
[ˈbrakəlɪ]
青花菜

8 cauliflower
[ˈkɔlɪˌflauɚ]
花椰菜

9 garlic
[ˈgarlɪk]
大蒜

3 mushroom
[ˈmʌʃrʊm]
菇

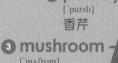

10 cucumber
[ˈkjukəmbɚ]
黃瓜

11 spinach
[ˈspɪnɪtʃ]
菠菜

12 asparagus
[əˈspærəgəs]
蘆筍

Let's make a vegetable salad.
我們來做蔬菜沙拉吧！

Vegetables

13 potato
[pə`teto]
馬鈴薯

14 lotus root
[`lotəs ˏrut]
蓮藕

15 Japanese radish
[`dʒæpəniz ˏrædɪʃ]
日本蘿蔔

16 carrot
[`kærət]
紅蘿蔔

17 pumpkin
[`pʌmpkɪn]
南瓜

18 green pepper
[grin] [`pɛpɚ]
青椒

19 eggplant
[`ɛgˏplænt]
茄子

20 tomato
[tə`meto]
番茄

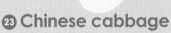

21 peas
[piz]
豌豆

22 leek
[lik]
韭蔥

23 Chinese cabbage
[`tʃaɪniz ˏkæbɪdʒ]
大白菜

24 sweet potato
[swit] [pə`teto]
番薯

25 celery
[`sɛlərɪ]
芹菜

26 bean sprouts
[`bin ˏspraʊts]
豆芽

27 corn
[kɔrn]
玉米

28 burdock
[`bɚˏdɑk]
牛蒡

Meals 1

[milz] [wʌn]

餐點 1

CD1
25

I had toast with jam.

我吃了烤吐司加果醬。

What did you have for breakfast?

你早餐吃了什麼？

❶ breakfast
[ˈbrɛkfəst]
早餐

❷ boiled egg
[bɔɪld] [ɛg]
水煮蛋

❸ sausage
[ˈsɔsɪdʒ]
香腸

❺ cereal
[ˈsɪrɪəl]
麥片

❻ jam
[dʒæm]
果醬

❹ bacon
[ˈbekən]
培根

❼ yogurt
[ˈjogɚt]
優格

❽ scrambled eggs
[ˈskræmbl̩d] [ɛgz]
炒蛋

❾ toast
[tost]
烤吐司

54

10 lunch
[ˈlʌntʃ]
午餐

11 sandwich
[ˈsændwɪtʃ]
三明治

12 dinner
[ˈdɪnɚ]
晚餐

13 curry and rice
[ˈkɝɪ] [ænd] [ˈraɪs]
咖哩飯

14 rice
[raɪs]
米飯

15 bread
[brɛd]
麵包

16 noodles
[ˈnudl̩z]
麵

17 egg
[ɛg]
蛋

18 cheese
[tʃiz]
起司

19 salad
[ˈsæləd]
沙拉

20 seafood
[ˈsiˌfud]
海鮮

22 chicken
[ˈtʃɪkən]
雞肉

23 pork
[pɔrk]
豬肉

24 beef
[bif]
牛肉

21 fish
[fɪʃ]
魚

25 meat
[mit]
肉

Meals 2
[milz] [tu]

餐點2

CD1
26

❶ **Menu** 菜單
[ˋmɛnju]

❷ **hamburger**
[ˋhæmbɝgɚ]
漢堡

❸ **hot dog**
[ˋhɑt ˏdɔg]
熱狗

❹ **French fries**
[frɛntʃ ˏfraɪz]
薯條

❺ **fried chicken**
[fraɪd] [ˋtʃɪkən]
炸雞

For here or to go?

內用還是外帶？

Good!!

To go, please.

外帶，麻煩您了。

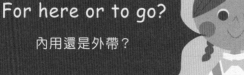

6 Chef's Recommendations
[ʃefs] [ˌrɛkəmɛnˋdeʃənz]
主廚推薦

7 pizza
[ˋpitsə]
披薩

8 soup
[sup]
湯

9 gratin
[ˋgrætən]
焗烤燉菜

10 omelet
[ˋɑmlɪt]
蛋包飯

11 steak
[stek]
牛排

12 potage
[pɔˋtɑʒ]
濃湯

13 spaghetti
[spəˋgɛtɪ]
義大利麵

14 beef stew
[bif] [stju]
燉牛肉

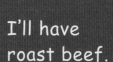

15 sautéed fish
[soˋted] [fɪʃ]
煎魚排

16 fried prawn
[fraɪd] [prɔn]
炸蝦

17 roast beef
[rost] [bif]
烤牛肉

Are you ready to order?

你準備好點餐了嗎？

I'll have roast beef.

我要點烤牛肉。

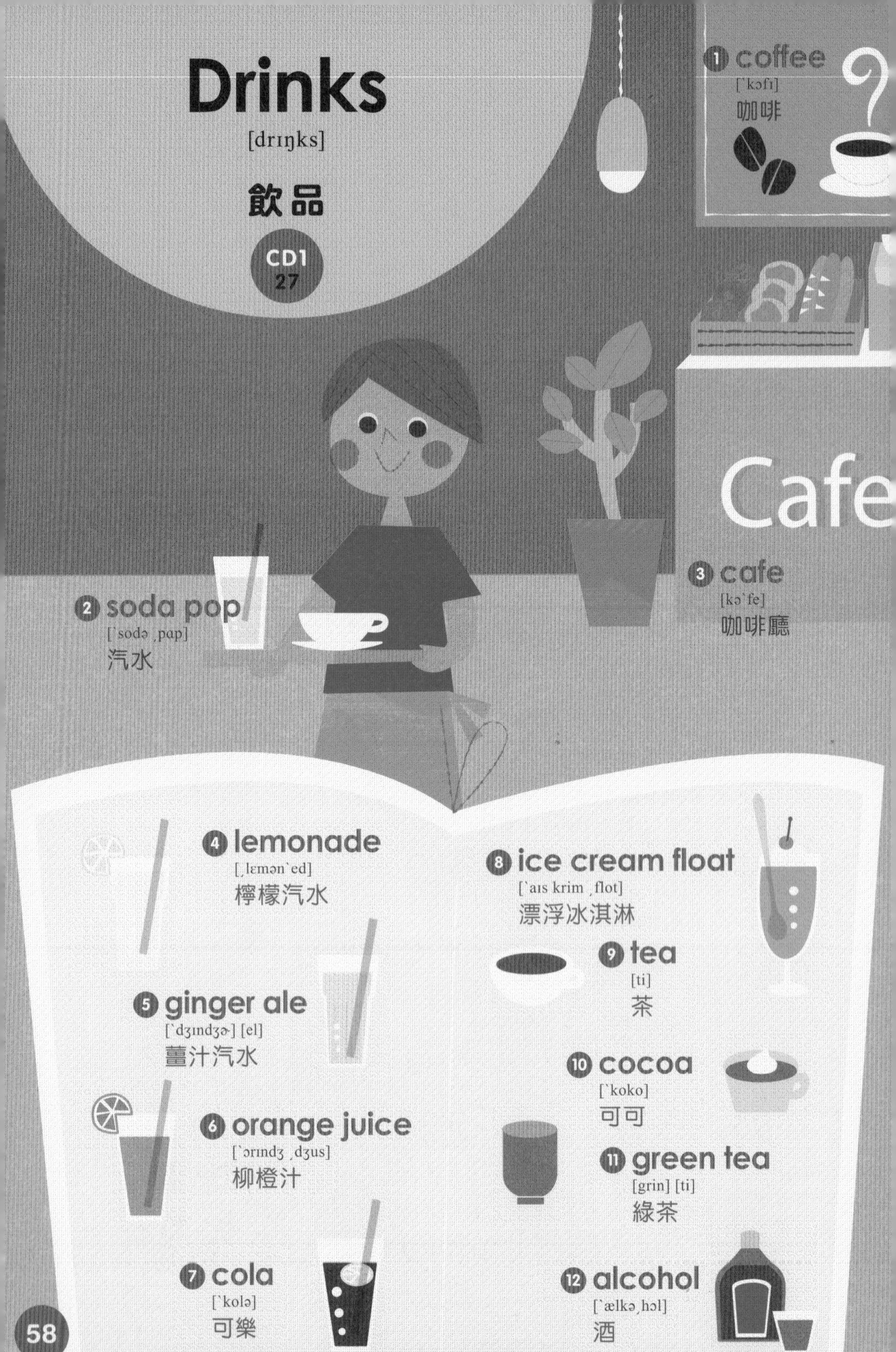

Drinks
[drɪŋks]
飲品
CD1
27
① coffee
[ˋkɔfɪ]
咖啡
Cafe
② soda pop
[ˋsodə ˏpɑp]
汽水
③ cafe
[kəˋfe]
咖啡廳
④ lemonade
[ˏlɛmənˋed]
檸檬汽水
⑤ ginger ale
[ˋdʒɪndʒɚ] [el]
薑汁汽水
⑥ orange juice
[ˋɔrɪndʒ ˏdʒus]
柳橙汁
⑦ cola
[ˋkolə]
可樂
⑧ ice cream float
[ˋaɪs krim ˏflot]
漂浮冰淇淋
⑨ tea
[ti]
茶
⑩ cocoa
[ˋkoko]
可可
⑪ green tea
[grin] [ti]
綠茶
⑫ alcohol
[ˋælkəˏhɔl]
酒

13 soy milk
[`sɔɪ͵mɪlk]
豆漿

14 milk
[mɪlk]
牛奶

What would you like to drink?

你想要點什麼飲料？

Orange juice, please.

柳橙汁，麻煩您了。

15 water
[`wɔtə]
水

16 cup
[kʌp]
杯子

17 glass
[ɡlæs]
玻璃杯

18 saucer
[`sɔsə]
茶托

19 straw
[strɔ]
吸管

20 mug
[mʌɡ]
馬克杯

Confectionery

[kən`fɛkʃən͵ɛrɪ]

甜點

CD1 28

I want ice cream, Mom.

我想要冰淇淋，媽媽。

ICE CREAM

❶ ice cream
[`aɪs ͵krim]
冰淇淋

Don't cry.

別哭。

2 lollipop
[ˋlɑlɪˌpɑp]
棒棒糖

3 candy
[ˋkændɪ]
糖果

4 jelly bean
[ˋdʒɛlɪˌbin]
雷根糖

5 chocolate
[ˋtʃɑkəlɪt]
巧克力

6 cupcake
[ˋkʌpˌkek]
杯子蛋糕

7 cake
[kek]
蛋糕

8 apple pie
[ˋæpḷ] [paɪ]
蘋果派

9 cheesecake
[ˋtʃizˌkek]
起司蛋糕

10 parfait
[parˋfe]
百匯、凍糕

11 custard pudding
[ˋkʌstəd ˌpʊdɪŋ]
焦糖布丁

12 jello
[ˋdʒɛlo]
果凍

13 pancake
[ˋpænˌkek]
鬆餅

14 donut
[ˋdoˌnʌt]
甜甜圈

15 crepe
[krep]
可麗餅

16 cracker
[ˋkrækə]
薄脆餅乾

17 cookie
[ˋkʊki]
餅乾

18 popcorn
[ˋpɑpˌkɔrn]
爆米花

19 potato chips
[pəˋteto ˌtʃɪps]
洋芋片

20 mashed sweet potatoes
[mæʃt] [swit] [pəˋtetoz]
番薯泥

Cooking
[`kʊkɪŋ]

料理

CD1 29

2 peel
[pil]
削、剝

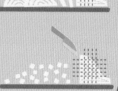

3 slice
[slaɪs]
切片

1 cut
[kʌt]
切

4 chop
[tʃɑp]
切碎

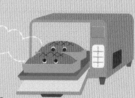

> **Let's make curry and rice.**
> 我們來做咖哩飯吧！

5 bake
[bek]
烘烤

> **I'll cook the rice.**
> 我來煮飯。

Curry

Curry

❻ grate
[gret]
磨碎

❼ mash
[mæʃ]
搗碎成泥

❽ boil
[bɔɪl]
烹煮、煮沸

❾ whip
[hwɪp]
攪打

❿ stir
[stɝ]
攪拌

⓫ pour
[por]
倒入

⓬ stew
[stju]
燉煮

⓭ fry
[fraɪ]
油煎

⓮ roast
[rost]
烘烤

⓯ grill
[grɪl]
（用烤架）燒烤

⓰ deep(-)fry
[ˈdip`fraɪ]
油炸

⓱ toast
[tost]
烤（麵包）

⓲ steam
[stim]
蒸

⓳ freeze
[friz]
冷凍

烹飪時常用的調味料和材料

⓴ sugar
[`ʃʊgɚ]
糖

㉑ salt
[sɔlt]
鹽

㉒ pepper
[`pɛpɚ]
胡椒

㉓ butter
[`bʌtɚ]
奶油

㉔ flour
[flaʊr]
麵粉

㉕ oil
[ɔɪl]
油

㉖ sauce
[sɔs]
醬料、醬油

㉗ ketchup
[`kɛtʃəp]
番茄醬

㉘ vinegar
[`vɪnɪgɚ]
醋

㉙ honey
[`hʌnɪ]
蜂蜜

與飲食相關的單字

介紹吃、喝、味道相關單字。

❶ eat
[it]
吃

❷ bite
[baɪt]
咬

❸ chew
[tʃu]
咀嚼

❹ lick
[lɪk]
舔

❺ drink
[drɪŋk]
喝

❻ bitter
[ˋbɪtɚ]
苦的

❼ sweet
[swit]
甜的

❽ hot
[hɑt]
熱的、辣的

❾ spicy
[ˋspaɪsɪ]
香料多的、辣的

❿ sour
[ˋsaʊr]
酸的

⓫ salty
[ˋsɔltɪ]
鹹的

⓬ delicious
[dɪˋlɪʃəs]
美味的

TOWN

[taʊn]

城鎮

In the City
[ɪn] [ðə] [`sɪtɪ]

在城市裡

CD1
31

❶ shrine
[ʃraɪn]
神社

❷ temple
[`tɛmpl]
寺廟

Where are you going?
你要去哪裡？

I'm going to the hospital.
我正要去醫院。

❹ apartment
[ə`partmənt]
公寓

❺ nursery school
[`nɝsərɪ ˏskul]
幼兒園、托兒所

❸ department store
[dɪ`partmənt ˏstor]
百貨公司

❻ school
[skul]
學校

❼ restaurant
[`rɛstərənt]
餐廳

❽ movie theater
[`muvɪ ˏθiətɚ]
電影院

❾ library
[`laɪˏbrɛrɪ]
圖書館

66

❿ factory
[`fæktərɪ]
工廠

⓫ stadium
[`stedɪəm]
體育場

⓬ station
[`steʃən]
車站

⓭ office building
[`ɔfɪs ˌbɪldɪŋ]
辦公大樓

⓮ city hall
[`sɪtɪ ˌhɔl]
市政府

⓯ post office
[`post ˌɔfɪs]
郵局

⓰ fire station
[`faɪr ˌsteʃən]
消防局

⓱ hospital
[`hɑspɪtl]
醫院

⓲ bank
[bæŋk]
銀行

⓳ police station
[pə`lis ˌsteʃən]
警察局

⓴ park
[park]
公園

㉑ hotel
[ho`tɛl]
飯店

㉒ museum
[mju`zɪəm]
博物館

㉓ church
[tʃɝtʃ]
教堂

67

Stores

[storz]

商店

CD1
32

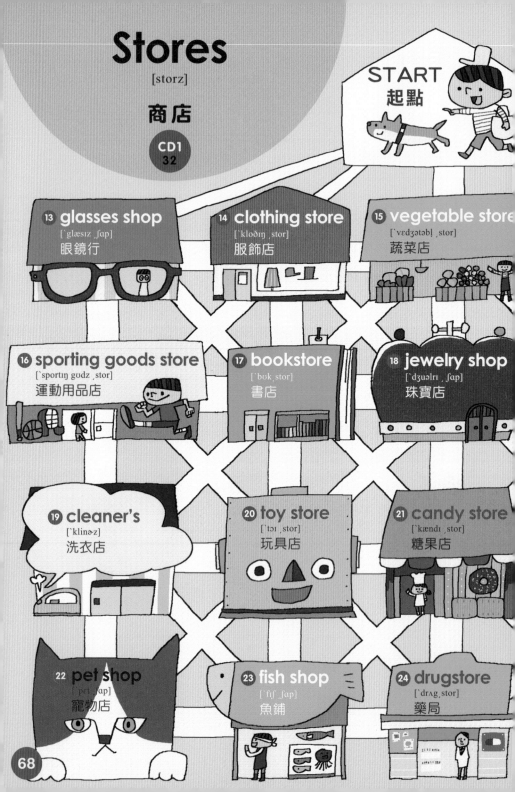

START
起點

13 glasses shop
[ˋglæsɪz ˏʃɑp]
眼鏡行

14 clothing store
[ˋkloðɪŋ ˏstor]
服飾店

15 vegetable store
[ˋvɛdʒətəbḻ ˏstor]
蔬菜店

16 sporting goods store
[ˋsportɪŋ gʊdz ˏstor]
運動用品店

17 bookstore
[ˋbʊk ˏstor]
書店

18 jewelry shop
[ˋdʒuəlrɪ ˏʃɑp]
珠寶店

19 cleaner's
[ˋklinɚz]
洗衣店

20 toy store
[ˋtɔɪ ˏstor]
玩具店

21 candy store
[ˋkændɪ ˏstor]
糖果店

22 pet shop
[ˋpɛt ˏʃɑp]
寵物店

23 fish shop
[ˋfɪʃ ˏʃɑp]
魚鋪

24 drugstore
[ˋdrʌg ˏstor]
藥局

68

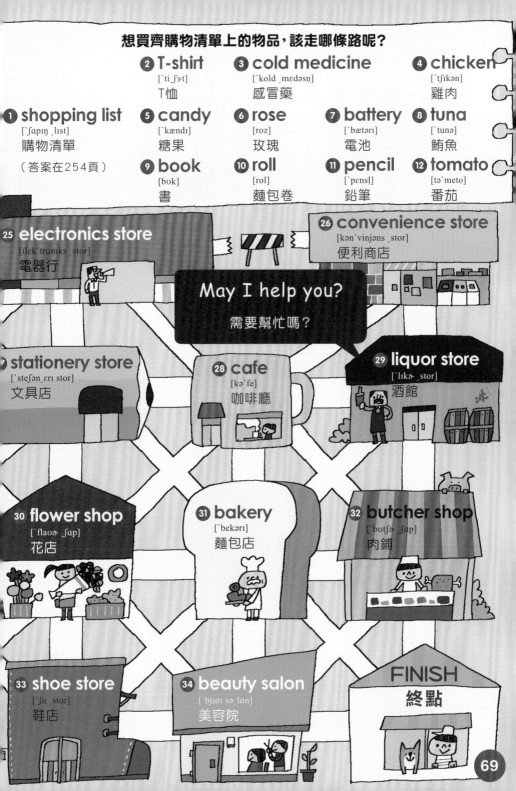

At the Supermarket

[æt] [ðə] [`supɚˌmɑrkɪt]

在超市裡

CD1
33

4 store clerk
[`stor ˌklɝk]
店員

3 seafood
[`siˌfud]
海鮮

5 fruit
[frut]
水果

2 meat
[mit]
肉

1 beverages
[`bɛvərɪdʒz]
飲料

7 eggs
[ɛgz]
蛋

6 vegetables
[`vɛdʒətəblz]
蔬菜

8 dairy products
[`dɛrɪ ˌprɑdəkts]
乳製品

MILK MILK

17 tasting samples
[`testɪŋ] [`sæmplz] 試吃

9 money
[`mʌnɪ]
錢

10 bill
[bɪl]
帳單

11 change
[tʃendʒ]
找零

12 coin
[kɔɪn]
硬幣

PIZZA
FOOD
PIZZA
FOOD
PIZZA

13 receipt
[rɪ`sit]
收據

18 frozen foods
[`frozn] [fudz]
冷凍食品

14 checkout counter
[`tʃɛkaʊt ˌkaʊntɚ]
收銀臺

15 checkout bag
[`tʃɛkaʊt ˌbæg]
購物袋

16 shopping basket
[`ʃɑpɪŋ ˌbæskɪt]
購物籃

70

19 bakery
[`bekərɪ]
麵包店

20 canned goods
[kænd] [gudz]
罐裝食品

21 shopping cart
[`ʃɑpɪŋ ˌkart]
購物手推車

23 sale
[sel]
出售、特賣

24 cosmetics
[kaz`mɛtɪks]
化妝品

**我要買的東西在哪裡？
一起找找看吧！**

27 shopping list
[`ʃɑpɪŋ ˌlɪst]
購物清單

28 banana
[bə`nænə]
香蕉

29 milk
[mɪlk]
牛奶

30 ham
[hæm]
火腿

31 chocolate
[`tʃɑkəlɪt]
巧克力

22 pet foods
[`pɛt ˌfudz]
寵物食品

Where can I find the cat food?
在哪裡可以找到貓飼料？

Over there.
在那邊。

25 snacks
[snæks]
零食

26 candy
[`kændɪ]
糖果

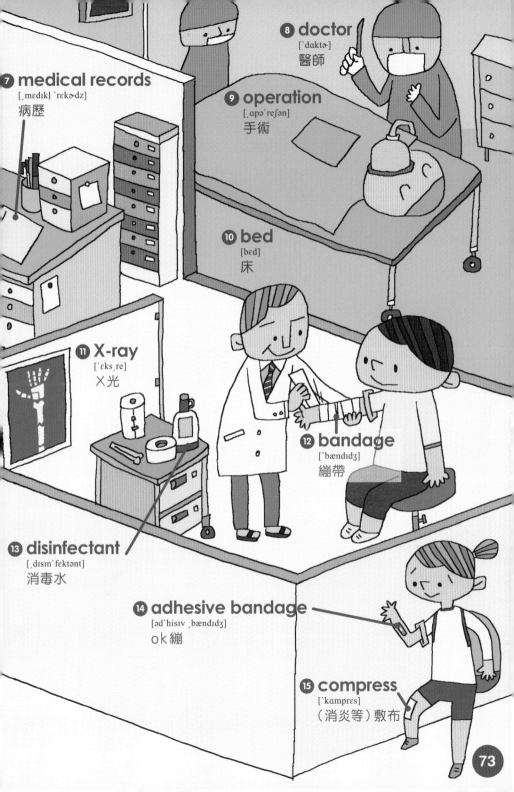

7 medical records
[ˌmɛdɪkḷ ˈrɛkɚdz]
病歷

8 doctor
[ˈdaktɚ]
醫師

9 operation
[ˌɑpəˈreʃən]
手術

10 bed
[bɛd]
床

11 X-ray
[ˈɛksˌre]
Ｘ光

12 bandage
[ˈbændɪdʒ]
繃帶

13 disinfectant
[ˌdɪsɪnˈfɛktənt]
消毒水

14 adhesive bandage
[ədˈhisɪv ˌbændɪdʒ]
ok 繃

15 compress
[ˈkɑmprɛs]
（消炎等）敷布

At the Park

[æt] [ðə] [park]

在公園裡

CD1 35

❶ play on the seesaw
[ple] [ɑn] [ðə] [ˋsiˌsɔ]
玩翹翹板

❷ seesaw
[ˋsiˌsɔ]
翹翹板

❸ walk the dog
[wɔk] [ðə] [dɔg]
遛狗

❹ bench
[bɛntʃ]
長凳

❺ slide
[slaɪd]
滑梯

❻ play on the slide
[ple] [ɑn] [ðə] [slaɪd]
溜滑梯

❼ sandbox
[ˋsændˌbɑks]
沙坑

❽ horizontal ba
[harəˋzɑntļ ˌbar]
單槓

❾ practice on a horizontal ba
[ˋpræktɪs] [ɑn] [ə] [harəˋzɑntļ ˌbar]
練習撐單槓

Roads
[rodz]

道路

CD1
36

⑤ tactile paving
[`tæktɪl ‚pevɪŋ]
導盲磚

④ dead end
[‚dɛd `ɛnd]
死路

① slope
[slop]
斜坡

② traffic accident
[`træfɪk ‚æksədənt]
交通事故

③ sign
[saɪn]
交通號誌

⑥ parking lot
[`parkɪŋ ‚lat]
停車場

truck

⑦ gas station
[`gæs ‚steʃən]
加油站

GAS STATION

⑨ manhole
[`mæn‚hol]
（下水道等供人出入的）人孔

⑧ traffic light
[`træfɪk ‚laɪt]
交通號誌燈

⑩ mailbo
[`mel‚baks]
郵筒

⑪ railroad crossing
[`rel‚rod] [`krɔsɪŋ]
鐵路平交道

⑫ crosswalk
[`krɔs‚wɔk]
行人穿越道

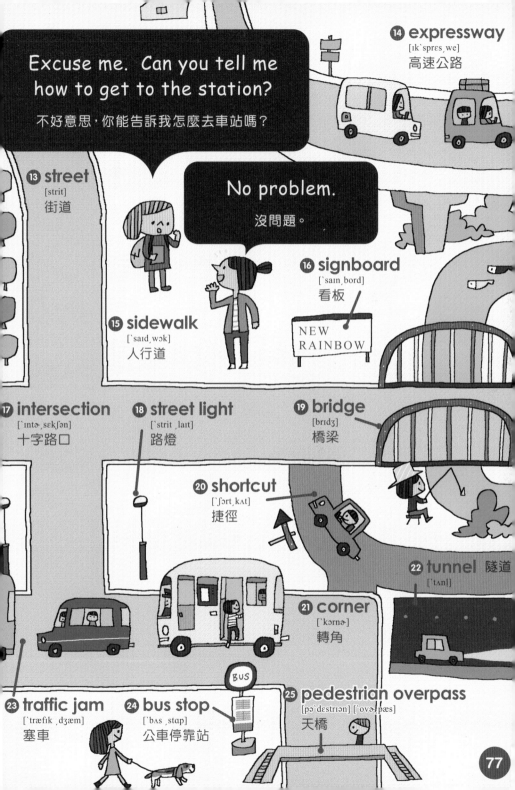

At the Station

[æt] [ðə] [`steʃən]

在車站裡

CD1 37

❶ **elevator**
[`ɛlə͵vetə]
電梯

❷ **driver**
[`draɪvə]
駕駛

❸ **train**
[tren]
火車

How many stops is
Kyoto Station from here?

請問從這裡到京都有多少站？

It's five stops from here.

距離這裡五站。

⑫ **track**
[træk]
軌道

⑬ **ticket**
[`tɪkɪt]
票、券

⑭ **smart card**
[`smart ͵kard]
IC卡

5 escalator
[`ɛskə͵letə˞]
電扶梯

9 door
[dor]
門

4 strap
[stræp]
拉環

8 seat
[sit]
座位

10 route map
[`rut ͵mæp]
路線圖

11 timetable
[`taɪm͵tebl]
時刻表

7 passenger
[`pæsn̩dʒə˞]
乘客

18 fare table
[`fɛr ͵tebl]
票價表

6 priority seat
[praɪ`ɔrətɪ ͵sit]
博愛座

17 information
[͵ɪnfə˞`meʃən]
服務臺

15 platform
[`plæt͵fɔrm]
月臺

16 ticket gate
[`tɪkɪt ͵get]
票閘

20 coin-operated locker
[`kɔɪn͵apə͵retɪd] [`lakə˞]
投幣式置物櫃

19 ticket machine
[`tɪkɪt mə͵ʃin]
售票機

79

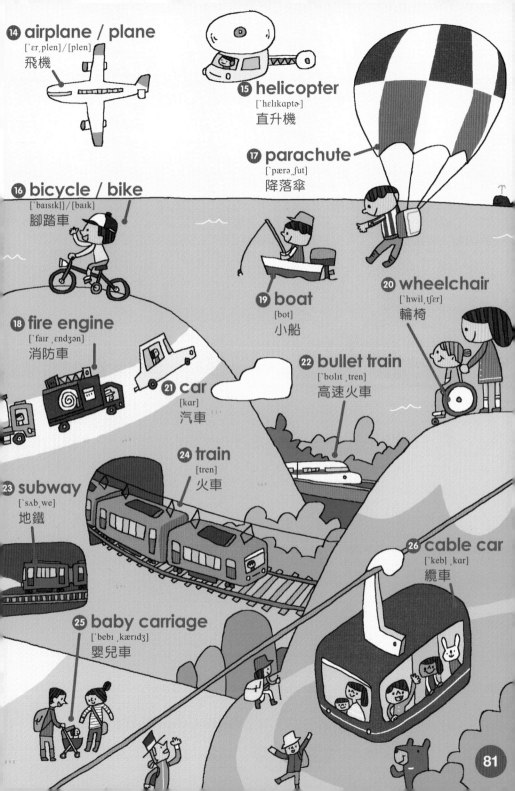

⓮ airplane / plane
[ˋɛrˏplen] / [plen]
飛機

⓯ helicopter
[ˋhɛlɪkɑptɚ]
直升機

⓰ bicycle / bike
[ˋbaɪsɪk!] / [baɪk]
腳踏車

⓱ parachute
[ˋpærəˏʃut]
降落傘

⓲ fire engine
[ˋfaɪr ˏɛndʒən]
消防車

⓳ boat
[bot]
小船

⓴ wheelchair
[ˋhwilˏtʃɛr]
輪椅

㉑ car
[kar]
汽車

㉒ bullet train
[ˋbʊlɪt ˏtren]
高速火車

㉔ train
[tren]
火車

㉓ subway
[ˋsʌbˏwe]
地鐵

㉖ cable car
[ˋkeb! ˏkar]
纜車

㉕ baby carriage
[ˋbebɪ ˏkærɪdʒ]
嬰兒車

Cars and Bicycles
[karz] [ænd] [`baɪsɪk!z]

汽車和腳踏車

CD1 39

3 car
[kɑr]
汽車

4 GPS
[ˌdʒi ˌpi `ɛs]
全球衛星定位系統

5 steering wheel
[`stɪrɪŋ ˌhwil]
方向盤

2 tricycle
[`traɪsɪk!]
三輪車

1 unicycle
[`junɪ ˌsaɪk!]
單輪車

9 passenger's seat
[`pæsn̩dʒɚz ˌsit]
副駕駛座

10 parking brake
[`parkɪŋ ˌbrek]
手煞車

11 driver's seat
[`draɪvɚz ˌsit]
駕駛座

12 door
[dor]
門

13 driver
[`draɪvɚ]
駕駛

14 wiper
雨刷

19 tire 輪胎
[taɪr]

82

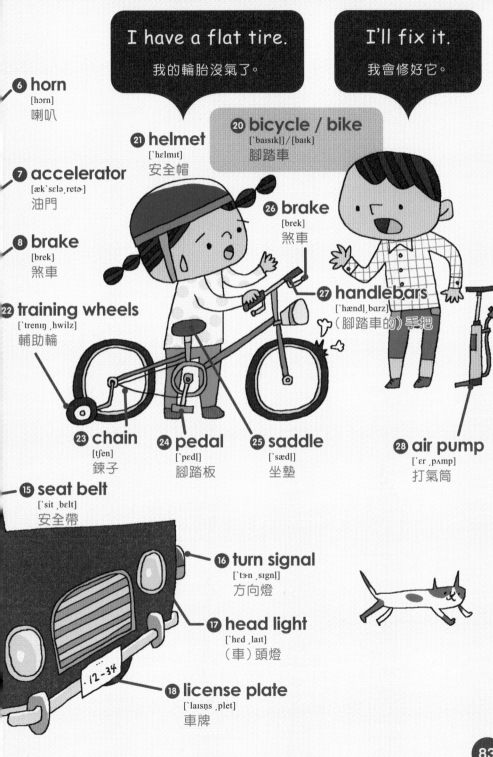

I have a flat tire.
我的輪胎沒氣了。

I'll fix it.
我會修好它。

6 horn
[hɔrn]
喇叭

21 helmet
[`hɛlmɪt]
安全帽

20 bicycle / bike
[`baɪsɪk!]/[baɪk]
腳踏車

7 accelerator
[æk`sɛlə͵retɚ]
油門

26 brake
[brek]
煞車

8 brake
[brek]
煞車

27 handlebars
[`hænd!͵barz]
（腳踏車的）手把

22 training wheels
[`trenɪŋ ͵hwilz]
輔助輪

23 chain
[tʃen]
鍊子

24 pedal
[`pɛd!]
腳踏板

25 saddle
[`sæd!]
坐墊

28 air pump
[`ɛr ͵pʌmp]
打氣筒

15 seat belt
[`sit ͵bɛlt]
安全帶

16 turn signal
[`tɝn ͵sɪgn!]
方向燈

17 head light
[`hɛd ͵laɪt]
（車）頭燈

18 license plate
[`laɪsn̩s ͵plet]
車牌

83

與交通工具相關的單字

CD1
40

關於使用火車、汽車、腳踏車等交通運輸工具的單字。

❶ buy a ticket
[baɪ] [ə] [ˋtɪkɪt]
購票

❷ get on a train
[ˌgɛt ˋɑn] [ə] [tren]
上火車

❸ get off a train
[ˌgɛt ˋɔf] [ə] [tren]
下火車

❹ wait for the train
[wet] [fɔr] [ðə] [tren]
等火車

❺ change trains
[tʃendʒ] [trenz]
轉乘火車

❻ drive a car
[draɪv] [ə] [kɑr]
開車（汽車）

❼ get into a car
[gɛt] [ɪntu] [ə] [kɑr]
上車（汽車）

❽ get out of a car
[gɛt] [aʊt] [əv] [ə] [kɑr]
下車（汽車）

❾ park a car
[pɑrk] [ə] [kɑr]
停車（汽車）

❿ ride a bicycle
[raɪd] [ə] [ˋbaɪsɪkl̩]
騎腳踏車

⓫ speed up
[spid ˋʌp]
加速

⓬ slow down
[slo ˋdaʊn]
減速

SCHOOL

[skul]

學校

School Rooms

[`skul ˌrumz]

校舍

CD1
41

❶ gym 體育館
[dʒɪm]

❺ library 圖書館
[`laɪˌbrɛrɪ]

❾ computer room
[kəm`pjutəˌrum]
電腦教室

❿ art room
[`artˌrum]
美術教室

❷ schoolyard
[`skulˌjard]
校園

❸ swimming pool
[`swɪmɪŋˌpul]
游泳池

❹ school gate
[`skulˌget]
校門

⑮ office 辦公室
[`ɔfɪs]

14 entrance
[`ɛntrəns]
入口

music room 音樂教室
['mjuzɪk ˌrum]

7 science room
['saɪəns ˌrum]
自然科學教室

8 nurse's room 保健室
['nɚsɪz ˌrum]

Good morning, everybody.

大家早安。

Good morning, Mr. Smith.

史密斯老師早安。

12 classroom
['klæs ˌrum]
教室

13 student
['stjudnt]
學生

11 teacher
['titʃɚ]
老師

16 teachers' room
['titʃɚz ˌrum]
教師辦公室

17 principal 校長
['prɪnsəpl]

19 restroom
['rɛst ˌrum]
洗手間

18 vice-principal
['vaɪs'prɪnsəpl]
副校長

通常男老師用「Mr.＋姓氏」稱呼，例如：Mr. Smith，
女老師用「Ms.＋姓氏」稱呼，例如：Ms. Smith。

87

School
[skul]

學校

CD1
42

學校的種類

❶ preschool 幼兒園
['pri,skul]

❷ kindergarten 幼兒園
['kɪndə,gartn] （通常為4～6歲幼兒）

❸ elementary school
[ɛlə'mɛntərɪ ,skul]
小學

❹ junior high school
['dʒunjə] ['haɪ ,skul]
國中

❺ high school
['haɪ ,skul]
高中

❻ college
['kalɪdʒ]
大學

❼ vocational school
[vo'keʃən ,skul]
職業學校

❽ junior college
['dʒunjə] ['kalɪdʒ]
專科學校

※本頁的路線僅為示例。

What grade are you in?
你念幾年級？

I'm in the third grade.
我念三年級。

❾ first grade 一年級
[fɝst] [gred]

❿ second grade 二年級
[ˋsɛkənd] [gred]

⓫ third grade 三年級
[θɝd] [gred]

⓬ fourth grade 四年級
[forθ] [gred]

⓭ fifth grade 五年級
[fɪfθ] [gred]

⓮ sixth grade 六年級
[sɪksθ] [gred]

⓯ enter
[ˋɛntɚ]
進入（入學）

⓰ graduate
[ˋgrædʒʊˏet]
畢業

⓱ diploma
[dɪˋplomə]
畢業證書

⓲ yearbook
[ˋjɪrˏbʊk]
畢業紀念冊

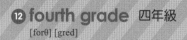

School Subjects
[`skul ˌsʌbdʒɪkts]

學習科目

CD1
43

學校的一天

❶ go to school
[go] [tu] [skul]
上學

❷ attend class
[ə`tɛnd] [klæs]
上課

❸ take a test
[tek] [ə] [tɛst]
考試

❹ have school lunch
[hæv] [`skul ˌlʌntʃ]
吃營養午餐

❺ Mandarin
[`mændərɪn]
國語

❻ Mathematics
[ˌmæθə`mætɪks]
數學

❿ Civics and Society
[`sɪvɪks] [ænd] [sə`saɪətɪ]
公民與社會

⓫ Arts
[arts]
藝術

⓰ Technology
[tɛk`nalədʒɪ]
科技

⓱ Calligraphy
[kə`lɪgrəfɪ]
書法

Oh, it's lunchtime.
噢！午餐時間到了。

That's all for today.
今天就教到這裡。

What subject do you like?
你喜歡哪個科目？

I like English.
我喜歡英語。

➐ Natural Sciences
[ˈnætʃərəl ˌsaɪənsɪs]
自然科學

➑ Social Studies
[ˈsoʃəl ˌstʌdɪz]
社會

➒ English
[ˈɪŋglɪʃ]
英語

⓬ Health and Physical Education
[hɛlθ] [ænd] [ˈfɪzɪkl] [ˌɛdʒʊˈkeʃən]
健康與體育

⓭ Geography
[dʒɪˈɑgrəfɪ]
地理

⓮ Integrative Activities
[ˈɪntəˌgretɪv ækˌtɪvətɪz]
綜合活動

⓯ Midday (Rest) Break
[ˈmɪdˌde (rɛst) ˈbrek]
午休時間

⓲ History
[ˈhɪstərɪ]
歷史

⓳ Class Meeting
[ˈklæs ˌmitɪŋ]
班會

⓴ Club Activities
[ˈklʌb ækˌtɪvətɪz]
社團活動

㉑ go home 回家
[go] [hom]

In the Classroom
[ɪn] [ðə] [ˈklæsˌrʊm]

在教室裡

CD1 44

① speake
[ˈspikɚ]
擴音機

> **Who knows the answer?**
> 誰知道答案？

③ shelf 架子
[ʃɛlf]

④ homeroom teacher
[ˈhomrum ˌtitʃɚ]
班級導師

⑨ handout
[ˈhændˌaʊt]
講義

⑪ desk
[dɛsk]
書桌

⑩ chair 椅子
[tʃɛr]

⑫ classmate 同學
[ˈklæsˌmet]

② **blackboard**
[ˈblæk‚bord]
黑板

⑦ **goal** 目標
[gol]

目標 充滿朝氣
的打招呼吧！

$$5 \times 5 = 25$$
$$3 \times 7 =$$

⑧ **thumbtack**
[ˈθʌm‚tæk]
圖釘

⑤ **chalk board eraser**
[ˈtʃɔk ‚bord] [ɪˈresɚ]
板擦

⑥ **chalk**
[tʃɔk]
粉筆

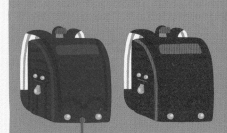

⑭ **textbook**
[ˈtɛkst‚bʊk]
教科書

⑮ **schoolbag**
[ˈskul‚bæg]
書包

⑬ **indoor shoes** 室內鞋
[ˈɪn‚dor] [ʃuz]

⑯ **drawer** 抽屜
[ˈdrɔɚ]

School Supplies

[ˋskul səˏplaɪz]

學用品

CD1 45

1 protractor
[proˋtræktə]
量角器

2 triangle
[ˋtraɪˏæŋgl]
三角板

3 report card
[rɪˋport ˏkɑrd]
成績單

4 journal
[ˋdʒɝnl]
日記

5 calculat
[ˋkælkjəˏletə]
計算機

6 box cutter 美工刀
[ˋbɑks ˏkʌtə]

7 packing tape
[ˋpækɪŋ ˏtep]
封箱膠帶

8 Scotch tape※
[ˋskɑtʃ ˏtep]
透明膠帶

9 abacus 算盤
[ˋæbəkəs]

10 compasses 圓規
[ˋkʌmpəsɪz]

11 stapler 訂書機
[ˋsteplə]

26 paint
[pent]
（用繪圖工具）繪畫

27 draw
[drɔ]
（畫圖或線條）繪畫

28 write 書寫
[raɪt]

29 erase 擦掉
[ɪˋres]

12 sticker 貼紙
[`stɪkə]

13 notebook
[`not͵bʊk]
筆記本

14 pencil case
[`pɛns͵ kes]
鉛筆盒

15 globe
[glob]
地球儀

17 pencil
[`pɛns]
鉛筆

18 eraser 橡皮擦
[ɪ`resə]

16 paper clip
[`pepə ͵klɪp]
迴紋針

19 ballpoint pen
[`bɔlpɔɪnt ͵pɛn]
原子筆

21 colored pencil 色鉛筆
[`kʌləd] [`pɛns]

20 scissors
[`sɪzəz]
剪刀

24 paint
[pent]
顏料

22 glue 膠水
[glu]

23 crayon 蠟筆
[`kreən]

25 pencil sharpener
[`pɛns ͵ʃɑrpənə]
削鉛筆機

※ Scotch tape是商標名稱。

30 paste 黏
[pest]

31 stick on 貼
[͵stɪk `ɑn]

32 cut 剪
[kʌt]

In the Science Room

[ɪn] [ðə] [ˈsaɪəns ˌrum]

在自然科學教室裡

CD1 46

1 **miniature bulb**
[ˈmɪnɪətʃə ˌbʌlb]
小燈泡

2 **dry battery** 乾電池
[draɪ] [ˈbætərɪ]

3 **astronomical telescope**
[ˌæstrəˈnamɪk!] [ˈtɛləˌskop]
天文望遠鏡

4 **beaker**
[ˈbikə]
燒杯

5 **flask**
[flæsk]
燒瓶

6 **dropper**
[ˈdrapə]
滴管

7 **liqui**
[ˈlɪkwɪd]
液體

8 **flam**
[flem]
火焰

9 **thermometer**
[θəˈmamətə]
溫度計

10 **gas burner**
[ˈgæs ˌbɜnə]
氣體燃燒器

magnifying glass 放大鏡
[`mægnə faɪŋ glæs]

It is fun to watch insects.

觀察昆蟲很有趣。

⑰ experiment 實驗
[ɪk`spɛrəmənt]

microscope
[`maɪkrə skop]
顯微鏡

⑱ observe 觀察
[əb`zɝv]

⑭ tweezers
[`twizɚz]
鑷子

⑬ powder 粉末
[`paʊdɚ]

⑮ magnet
[`mægnɪt]
磁鐵

⑯ test tube 試管
[`tɛst tjub]

⑲ discover 發現
[dɪs`kʌvɚ]

In the Music Room
[ɪn] [ðə] [ˈmjuzɪk ˌrum]

在音樂教室裡

CD1 47

❶ cymbal
[ˈsɪmbl̩z]
鈸

❷ piano
[pɪˈæno]
鋼琴

Let's sing a song

來唱首歌吧！

❸ chorus
[ˈkorəs]
合唱、
合唱團

Suzy plays the piano very well.

蘇西彈了一手好琴。

❹ tambourine
[ˌtæmbəˈrin]
鈴鼓

❺ castanets
[ˈkæstəˌnɛts]
響板

❻ accordion
[əˈkɔrdɪən]
手風琴

❼ harmonica
[harˈmanɪkə]
口琴

 **❽ recorder** 直笛
[rɪˈkɔrdɚ]

 **❾ conductor** 指揮家
[kənˈdʌktɚ]

98

10 snare drum
[snɛr] [drʌm]
小鼓

11 bass drum 大鼓
[bes] [drʌm]

12 drums 鼓
[drʌmz]

14 violin
[ˌvaɪəˈlɪn]
小提琴

15 xylophone
[ˈzaɪləˌfon]
木琴

13 guitar
[gɪˈtar]
吉他

16 maracas
[məˈrækəz]
沙鈴

17 French horn
[frɛntʃ] [hɔrn]
法國號

18 trombone
[tramˈbon]
長號

19 trumpet
[ˈtrʌmpɪt]
小號

22 reed organ
[ˈrid ˈɔrgən]
簧風琴

20 flute
[flut]
長笛

21 clarinet
[ˌklærɪˈnɛt]
單簧管

99

In the Library
[ɪn] [ðə] [ˈlaɪˌbrɛrɪ]

在圖書館裡

CD1 48

1 librarian 圖書館員
[laɪˈbrɛrɪən]

2 circulation desk
[ˌsɝˈkjəˈleʃən ˌdɛsk]
借書處

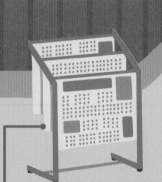

9 dictionary
[ˈdɪkʃənˌɛrɪ]
字典

10 illustrated book 圖鑑
[ˈɪləstretɪd] [bʊk]

11 picture book 圖書
[ˈpɪktʃɚ ˌbʊk]

12 biography
[baɪˈɑgrəfɪ]
傳記

13 magazine
[ˈmægəˌzin]
雜誌

14 fairy tale
[ˈfɛrɪ ˌtelz]
童話故事

3 newspaper
[ˈnjuzˌpepɚ]
報紙

6 page
[pedʒ]
頁

4 book
[bʊk]
書

5 cover 封面
[ˈkʌvɚ]

7 table of contents 目次
[ˈtebl] [əv] [ˈkɑntɛnts]

8 index 索引
[ˈɪndɛks]

comic

comic book
[`kamɪk ˌbʊk]
漫畫書

16 fiction
story 小說
[`fɪkʃən ˌstorɪ]

photograph
collection
[`fotəˌɡræf kə`lɛkʃən]
寫真集

18 reference
book
[`rɛfərəns ˌbʊk]
參考書

19 read 閱讀
[rid]

20 borrow
[`baro]
借

21 return
[rɪ`tɝn]
歸還

This book is
very interesting.

這本書十分有趣。

Can I borrow it? 我可以借閱嗎？

與學習相關的單字

CD1
49

介紹學校生活常用單字、片語。

❶ study
[ˋstʌdɪ]
學習、研讀

❷ think
[θɪŋk]
思考

❸ read
[rid]
閱讀

❹ write
[raɪt]
書寫

❺ calculate
[ˋkælkjəˌlet]
計算

❻ copy
[ˋkɑpɪ]
抄寫、複製

❼ ask a question
[æsk] [ə] [ˋkwɛstʃən]
提問

❽ answer
[ˋænsɚ]
回答

❾ discuss
[dɪˋskʌs]
討論

❿ give a presentation
[gɪv] [ə] [ˌprɛzn̩ˋteʃən]
發表

⓫ turn in
[ˌtɝn ˋɪn]
繳交

⓬ raise my hand
[rez] [maɪ] [hænd]
舉手

NATURE

[ˋnetʃə]

大自然

Animals 1

[ˈænəm|z] [wʌn]

動物 1

CD2 02

介紹動物園裡的動物。

1 **giraffe**
[dʒəˈræf]
長頸鹿

2 **deer**
[dɪr]
鹿

3 **kangaroo**
[ˌkæŋɡəˈru]
袋鼠

4 **donkey**
[ˈdɑŋkɪ]
驢子

5 **zebra**
[ˈzibrə]
斑馬

6 **cheetah**
[ˈtʃitə]
獵豹

7 **leopard**
[ˈlɛpəd]
豹

8 **elephant**
[ˈɛləfənt]
象

9 **bea**
[bɛr]
熊

10 **rhinoceros** 犀牛
[raɪˈnɑsərəs]

11 **tiger**
[ˈtaɪɡə]
老虎

12 **koala**
[koˈɑlə]
無尾熊

13 **squirrel**
[ˈskwɜ·əl]
松鼠

14 **bat**
[bæt]
蝙蝠

15 **pandɑ**
[ˈpændə]
貓熊

Animals 2

[ˋænəm[z] [tu]

動物2

CD2
03

這些是農場裡的動物。

1 hay
[he]
乾草

2 bull 公牛
[bʊl]

3 rat
[ræt]
老鼠

4 calf
[kæf]
小牛

5 cow 母牛
[kaʊ]

6 mole
[mol]
鼴鼠

7 turkey
[ˋtɝkɪ]
火雞

8 pasture
[ˋpæstʃɚ]
牧場、牧草地

9 duck
[dʌk]
鴨

10 goose
[gus]
鵝

11 frog
[frag]
青蛙

Animals 3

[ˋænəmḷz] [θri]

動物3

CD2
04

這些動物是最有人氣的寵物。

❶ goldfish
[ˋgoldˌfɪʃ]
金魚

Feed me.
餵我。

❷ parrot
[ˋpærət]
鸚鵡

❹ tortoise
[ˋtɔrtəs]
龜、陸龜

❸ parakeet
[ˋpærəˌkit]
長尾鸚鵡

Bowwow!
汪汪!

❺ dog
[dɔg]
狗

Birds
[bɝdz]

鳥

CD2
05

1 cuckoo
[ˋkʊku]
布穀鳥

2 pigeon
[ˋpɪdʒɪn]
鴿子

3 sparrow
[ˋspæro]
麻雀

4 seagull
[ˋsi gʌl]
海鷗

5 eagle
[ˋigl]
老鷹

Did you know that penguins can't fly?

你知道企鵝不會飛嗎？

Really?

真的嗎？

6 pheasant
[ˋfɛznt]
雉雞

7 penguin
[ˋpɛngwɪn]
企鵝

8 pelican
[ˋpɛlɪkən]
鵜鶘

9 swan
[swɑn]
天鵝

⑩ swallow
[`swalo]
燕子

⑪ hawk
[hɔk]
較小的鷹科和
較大的隼科鳥類

與鳥相關的單字

⑲ cage
[kedʒ]
籠子

㉑ wing
[wɪŋ]
翅膀

⑳ bill / beak
[bɪl] / [bik]
喙

⑫ nest
[nɛst]
巢

⑭ woodpecker
[`wʊd͵pɛkə]
啄木鳥

⑮ crane
[kren]
鶴

⑬ owl
[aʊl]
貓頭鷹

⑯ flamingo
[flə`mɪŋgo]
紅鶴

⑰ peacock
[`pikɑk]
孔雀

⑱ ostrich
[`ɑstrɪtʃ]
鴕鳥

Insects

[`ɪnsɛkts]

昆蟲

**CD2
06**

除了昆蟲，還介紹了其他常見的小生物。

4 moth
[mɔθ]
蛾

3 caterpillar
[`kætə‚pɪlə]
毛蟲

2 beetle
[bitl]
甲蟲

1 web
[wɛb]
網

7 honeycomb
[`hʌnɪ‚kom]
蜂巢

9 mosquito
[məs`kito]
蚊子

8 bee
[bi]
蜜蜂

6 stag beetle
[`stæg ‚bitl]
鍬形蟲

10 honey
[`hʌnɪ]
蜂蜜

11 snail
[snel]
蝸牛

5 spider
[`spaɪdə]
蜘蛛

12 ant
[ænt]
螞蟻

13 praying mantis
[`preɪŋ ‚mæntɪs]
螳螂

14 butterfly.
[ˈbʌtə‿ˌflaɪ]
蝴蝶

15 dragonfly
[ˈdrægən‿ˌflaɪ]
蜻蜓

與昆蟲相關的單字

25 pupa
[ˈpjupə]
蛹

26 wing
[wɪŋ]
翅膀

27 larva
[ˈlɑrvə]
幼蟲

16 cicada
[sɪˈkadə]
蟬

Wow! I caught a grasshopper!
哇！我抓到一隻蚱蜢！

17 longicorn
[ˈlandʒə‿ˌkɔrn]
天牛

18 gecko
[ˈgɛko]
壁虎

19 ladybug
[ˈledɪ‿ˌbʌg]
瓢蟲

20 grasshopper
[ˈgræs‿ˌhapə]
蚱蜢

22 toad
[tod]
蟾蜍

23 water strider
[ˈwɔtə‿ˌstraɪdə]
水黽

21 firefly
[ˈfaɪr‿ˌflaɪ]
螢火蟲

24 earthworm
[ˈɝθ‿ˌwɝm]
蚯蚓

Ocean Fish

[`oʃən ˌfɪʃ]

海裡的魚

CD2
07

這裡集合了海中的魚類和生物。

1 shark
[ʃark]
鯊魚

2 shellfish
[`ʃɛl ˌfɪʃ]
貝

3 sea otter
[`si ˌatɚ]
海獺

4 ray
[re]
魟魚

5 blowfish
[`blo ˌfɪʃ]
河魨

6 sardine
[sarˋdin]
沙丁魚

7 whale
[hwel]
鯨魚

8 sunfish
[`sʌn ˌfɪʃ]
翻車魚

9 porgy
[`pɔrgɪ]
鯛魚

10 seaweed
[`si ˌwid]
海藻

11 starfish 海星
[`star ˌfɪʃ]

12 sea anemone
[`si ə ˌnɛmənɪ]
海葵

13 sea urchin
[`si ˌɝtʃɪn]
海膽

14 crab
[kræb]
蟹

Where is the treasure of the sea?

大海的寶物在哪裡？

（答案在254頁）

114

5 sea
[si]
海洋

16 turtle
['tɝtḷ]
海龜、龜

17 tuna
['tunə]
鮪魚

18 dolphin
['dɑlfən]
海豚

19 octopus
['ɑktəpəs]
章魚

20 seal
[sil]
海豹

21 sea horse
['si ˌhɔrs]
海馬

22 squid
[skwɪd]
烏賊、魷魚

23 jellyfish
['dʒɛlɪˌfɪʃ]
水母

24 shrimp
[ʃrɪmp]
蝦

25 flatfish
['flæt fɪʃ]
比目魚

26 angler
['æŋglɚ]
鮟鱇魚

27 prawn
[prɔn]
明蝦

River Fish
[ˈrɪvɚ ˌfɪʃ]

河川裡的魚

CD2 08

這裡聚集河川及池子裡的魚類和生物。

和魚相關的單字

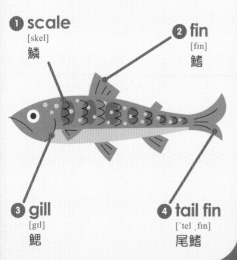

1 scale
[skel]
鱗

2 fin
[fɪn]
鰭

3 gill
[gɪl]
鰓

4 tail fin
[ˈtel ˌfɪn]
尾鰭

5 carp
[karp]
鯉魚

6 crucian carp
[ˈkruʃən ˌkarp]
鯽魚

7 trout
[traʊt]
鱒魚

8 eel
[il]
鰻魚

9 catfish
[ˈkæt ˌfɪʃ]
鯰魚

Flowers
[`flaʊəz]

花

CD2
09

① **cactus**
[`kæktəs]
仙人掌

② **iris**
[`aɪrɪs]
鳶尾花

③ **sunflower**
[`sʌn͵flaʊə]
向日葵

④ **rape blossom**
[rep] [`blɑsəmz]
油菜花

⑤ **morning glory**
[`mɔrnɪŋ] [`glɔrɪ]
牽牛花

⑥ **dandelion**
[`dændɪ͵laɪən]
蒲公英

⑦ **cosmos**
[`kazməs]
波斯菊

⑧ **rose**
[roz]
玫瑰

⑨ **carnation**
[kar`neʃən]
康乃馨

⑩ **dahlia**
[`daljə]
大理菊

⑪ **viole**
[`vaɪəlɪt]
紫羅蘭

⑫ **lily**
[`lɪlɪ]
百合

⑬ **orchid**
[`ɔrkɪd]
蘭花

What flower is this?
這是什麼花？

It's a rose.
這是玫瑰。

cherry blossoms
[ˋtʃɛrɪ] [ˋblɑsəmz]
櫻花

daffodil
[ˋdæfədɪl]
水仙

16 tulip
[ˋtjuləp]
鬱金香

17 daisy
[ˋdezɪ]
雛菊

poppy
[ˋpɑpɪ]
罌粟

19 lily of the valley
[ˋlɪlɪ] [əv] [ðə] [ˋvælɪ]
鈴蘭

20 chrysanthemum
[krɪˋsænθəməm]
菊花

21 hydrangea
[haɪˋdrɛndʒə]
繡球花

和植物相關的單字

22 petal
[ˋpɛtl]
花瓣

23 bud
[bʌd]
花蕾、芽

24 leaf
[lif]
葉子

25 thorn
[θɔrn]
刺

26 stem
[stɛm]
莖

27 root
[rut]
根

28 bulb
[bʌlb]
球莖

29 seed
[sid]
種子

30 tree 樹
[tri]

31 twig
[twɪg]
細枝

32 branch
[bræntʃ]
樹枝

33 trunk
[trʌŋk]
樹幹

34 vine
[vaɪn]
藤、蔓

At the Beach
[æt] [ðə] [ˋbitʃ]

在海灘

CD2
10

從線索中找到隱藏
在海邊的犯人！

（答案在254頁）

線索
1

He's wearing sunglasses.
他戴著太陽眼鏡。

❶ **lighthouse**
[ˋlaɪt͵haʊs]
燈塔

❷ **surfer**
[ˋsɝ·fɚ]
衝浪者

❹ **snorkel**
[ˋsnɔrkḷ]
潛水呼吸管設

❸ **swim ring**
[ˋswɪm ͵rɪŋ]
游泳圈

❽ **seashell**
[ˋsi ͵ʃɛl]
貝殼

❼ **sandcastle**
[ˋsænd͵kæsḷ]
沙堡

❺ **beach umbrella**
[ˋbitʃ ʌm ͵brɛlə]
（海灘等處）遮陽傘

❾ **sunglasses**
[ˋsʌn͵glæsɪz]
太陽眼鏡

UV CUT
❻ **sunscreen**
[ˋsʌn͵skrin]
防晒乳

❿ **sand**
[sænd]
沙

線索 2
He's wearing green swimming trunks.
他穿著綠色的泳褲。

線索 3
He likes shaved ice.
他喜歡刨冰。

12 **horizon**
[həˈraɪzn̩]
水平線

14 **shore**
[ʃɔr]
海岸

1 **wave**
[wev]
海浪

13 **rock**
[rak]
岩石

16 **seawater**
[ˈsiˌwɔtɚ]
海水

15 **swimmer**
[ˈswɪmɚ]
游泳者

20 **shaved ice**
[ˌʃevd ˈaɪs]
刨冰

17 **beach ball**
[ˈbitʃ ˌbɔl]
海灘球

19 **swimsuit**
[ˈswɪmsut]
泳衣

18 **swimming trunks**
[ˈswɪmɪŋ ˌtrʌŋks]
泳褲

21 **lifeguard**
[ˈlaɪfˌgard]
救生員

22 **beach**
[bitʃ]
海灘

121

In the Country
[ɪn] [ðə] [ˈkʌntrɪ]

在鄉間

CD2
11

❹ rainbow 彩虹
[ˈren͵bo]

❺ volcano
[vɑlˈkeno]
火山

❶ cliff
[klɪf]
懸崖

❸ rice field
[ˈraɪs ͵fild]
稻田

❷ stream
[strim]
河流

❼ hammock
[ˈhæmək]
吊床

❻ campsite
[ˈkæmp͵saɪt]
露營地

❾ sleeping bag
[ˈslipɪŋ ͵bæg]
睡袋

❽ tent
[tɛnt]
帳篷

We're almost at the summit

我們快到山頂了。

Mom, I'm hungry.

媽媽，我餓了。

❿ backpack
[ˈbæk͵pæk]
背包

12 echo [`ɛko] 回音

Hello!
Hello!

11 summit [`sʌmɪt] 山頂

14 cave [kev] 洞穴

16 valley 山谷 [`vælɪ]

13 orchard [`ɔrtʃəd] 果園

17 waterfall [`wɔtə‚fɔl] 瀑布

15 forest 森林 [`fɔrɪst]

20 field [fild] 田地

18 woods 樹林 [wʊdz]

19 mountain hut [`maʊntn̩ ‚hʌt] 山間小屋

21 hill 小丘、丘陵 [hɪl]

23 tunnel [`tʌnl̩] 隧道

22 grass [græs] 草

24 lake [lek] 湖泊

Space

[spes]

宇宙

CD2 12

3 rocket
火箭

4 astronaut
太空人

5 **sun**
[sʌn]
太陽

11 comet
[`kamɪt]
彗星

9 moon
[mun]
月球

10 Mars
[mɑrz]
火星

8 Earth
[ɝθ]
地球

6 Mercury
[`mɝkjərɪ]
水星

7 Venus
[`vinəs]
金星

16 orbit
[`ɔrbɪt]
軌道

2 July 19, 2017
2017年7月19日

We met an alien.
我們遇見了一位外星人。

He is very nice. We are friends now.
他人非常好。我們現在是好朋友。

17 alien
[`elɪən]
外星人

18 shooting star
[`ʃutɪŋ star]
流星

肯的宇宙旅行日記

1 July 18, 2017
2017年7月18日
We saw the earth.
我們看見地球了。
The earth was blue and beautiful.
地球又藍又美麗。

各種月亮的形狀

25 full moon
[fol] [mun]
滿月

26 half-moon
[`hæf ˌmun]
半月

27 crescent moon
[`krɛsnt] [mun]
眉月

13 Saturn
[`sætɚn]
土星

14 Uranus
[jʊˈrenəs]
天王星

15 Neptune
[`nɛptjun]
海王星

Jupiter
[`dʒupətɚ]
木星

22 Milky Way
[`mɪlkɪ we]
銀河

19 North Star
[nɔrθ stɑr]
北極星

21 Big Dipper
[bɪɡ `dɪpɚ]
北斗七星

23 Telescope
[`tɛlə skop]
望遠鏡

24 star
[stɑr]
星星

Constellation
[ˌkɑnstə`leʃən]
星座

The Weather

[ðə] [ˈwɛðə·]

天氣

湯姆的天氣插圖日記

❶ It's sunny.
[ɪts] [ˈsʌnɪ]
晴朗的

❷ It's stormy.
[ɪts] [ˈstɔrmɪ]
暴風雨的

❹ It's cloudy.
[ɪts] [ˈklaʊdɪ]
多雲的

❺ It's humi
[ɪts] [ˈhjumɪd]
潮溼的

❼ It's rainy.
[ɪts] [ˈrenɪ]
多雨的

❽ It's fogg
[ɪts] [ˈfɑgɪ]
有霧的

❿ It's snowy.
[ɪts] [ˈsnoɪ]
下雪的

⓫ It's wind
[ɪts] [ˈwɪn
風大

How is the weather today?

今天天氣如何？

It's hot. 炎熱的
[ɪts] [hɑt]

It's cold.
[ɪts] [kold]

寒冷的

❾ It's warm. 溫暖的
[ɪts] [wɔrm]

It's freezing.
[ɪts] [ˋfrizɪŋ]

冰凍的

與天氣相關的單字

❽ cloud
[klaʊd]
雲

❼ rain
[ren]
雨

❺ rainbow
[ˋrenˌbo]
彩虹

❻ snow
[sno]
雪

❼ wind
[wɪnd]
風

❽ storm
[stɔrm]
暴風雨

❾ typhoon
[taɪˋfun]
颱風

❷⓿ thunder
[ˋθʌndɚ]
雷

127

與貓狗相關的單字

CD2
14

介紹人氣寵物貓、狗相關的單字。

❶ paw
[pɔ]
腳掌、爪

❼ scratch
[skrætʃ]
抓

❷ whiskers
[ˋhwɪskəz]
鬍鬚

❽ Sit!
[sɪt]
坐下！

❸ claw
[klɔ]
爪

❾ Down!
[daʊn]
趴下！

❹ tail
[tel]
尾巴

❿ Beg!
[bɛg]
拜託！

❺ bark
[bark]
吠叫

⓫ Stay!
[ste]
等等！

❻ groom
[grum]
（寵物）美容、整潔梳理

⓬ Give me your paw!
[gɪv] [mi] [jʊə] [pɔ]
握手！

SPORTS
[spɔrts]

and
[ænd]

AMUSEMENTS
[ə`mjuzmənts]

運動和娛樂

Outdoor Games
[`aʊtˌdor] [gemz]

戶外遊戲

CD2
15

What do you want to play?

你想要玩什麼？

I want to play kick-the-can.

我想玩踢罐子。

❷ ride a unicycle
[raɪd] [ə] [`junɪˌsaɪkl]
騎單輪車

❶ play kick-the-can
[ple] [ˌkɪk ðə `kæn]
玩踢罐子

❸ play tag
[ple] [tæg]
玩鬼捉人

❹ play hide-and-seek
[ple] [`haɪd n ˌsik]
玩躲貓貓

⑤ play dodgeball
[ple] [`dadʒˌbɔl]
玩躲避球

⑥ roller-skate
[`roləˌsket]
（輪式）溜冰

⑦ play cops and robbers
[ple] [`kɑps ən ˌrɑbəⴰz]
玩官兵捉強盜

⑧ jump rope
[dʒʌmp] [rop]
跳繩

⑨ ride a skateboard
[raɪd] [ə] [`sketˌbord]
溜滑板

⑩ blow bubbles
[blo] [`bʌblz]
吹泡泡

131

Indoor Games

[`ɪn͵dor] [gemz]

室內遊戲

❶ play rock-paper-scissors
[ple] [͵rak ͵pepɚ `sɪzɚz]
猜拳

Rock, paper, scissors.

剪刀、石頭、布。

rock表示石頭，paper表示布，scissors表示剪刀。

❷ play with blocks
[ple] [wɪð] [blaks]
堆積木

❸ do origami
[du] [͵ɔrə`gamɪ]
摺紙

❹ play ringtoss
[ple] [`rɪŋ͵tɔs]
玩套圈圈

❺ play cards
[ple] [kardz]
玩紙牌

6 do a jigsaw puzzle
[du] [ə] [`dʒɪg͵sɔ ͵pʌzl]
拼拼圖

7 play bingo
[ple] [`bɪŋgo]
玩賓果遊戲

8 play musical chairs
[ple] [`mjuzɪkl] [tʃɛrz]
玩搶椅子

10 do a crossword puzzle
[du] [ə] [`krɔswɚd ͵pʌzl]
做填字遊戲

9 play with a yo-yo
[ple] [wɪð] [ə] [`jo͵jo]
玩溜溜球

11 play with dolls
[`ple] [wɪð] [dɑlz]
玩洋娃娃、玩玩偶

133

Toys
[tɔɪz]

玩具

CD2
17

平安夜那天
聖誕老人會有我想要的東西嗎？

❸ **robot**
[`robət]
機器人

❶ **stuffed animal**
[,stʌft `ænəml]
（動物造型）填充娃娃

❷ **video game**
[`vɪdɪo ,gem]
電玩遊戲

❺ **jump rope**
[`dʒʌmp ,rop]
跳繩

❻ **jack-in-the-box**
[`dʒæk ɪn ðə ,baks]
玩偶盒、驚喜盒

❹ **toy car**
[`tɔɪ ,kar]
玩具車

❼ **doll**
[dɑl]
洋娃娃、
玩偶

❽ **water pistol**
[`wɔtɚ ,pɪstl]
水槍

❾ **radio-controlled car**
[,redɪo kən`trold] [kar]
遙控汽車

I want a robot.

我想要一個機器人。

10 jigsaw puzzle
[ˈdʒɪgˌsɔ ˌpʌzl]
拼圖

11 kite
[kaɪt]
風箏

13 trampoline
[ˌtræmpəˈlin]
彈跳床

12 figurine
[ˌfɪgjəˈrin]
模型

14 teddy bear
[ˈtɛdɪ ˌbɛr]
泰迪熊

15 cards
[kardz]
紙牌

16 drone
[dron]
無人機

17 hula hoop
[ˈhulə ˌhup]
呼拉圈

18 dice
[daɪs]
骰子

19 piggy bank
[ˈpɪgɪ ˌbæŋk]
小豬撲滿

21 slime
[slaɪm]
黏土

20 yo-yo
[ˈjoˌjo]
溜溜球

Language Games
[ˈlæŋgwɪdʒ ˌgemz]

文字遊戲

CD2
18

❶ word chain game 文字接龍遊戲
[ˈwɝd tʃen ˌgem]

| cap
[kæp]
棒球帽 | → | pen
[pɛn]
原子筆 | → | notebook
[ˈnot͵bʊk]
筆記本 | → | knife
[naɪf]
刀子 | → | egg
[ɛg]
蛋 |

❷ crossword puzzle
[ˈkrɔsˌwɝd ˌpʌzl]
填字遊戲

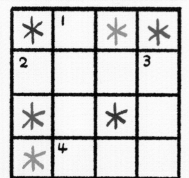

（答案在254頁）

DOWN 縱向
[daʊn]

1. A large fish that lives in lakes and rivers.
生活在湖泊和河流中的大型魚類。

3. It says "Bowwow."
牠會發出「汪汪」聲。

ACROSS 橫向
[əˈkrɔs]

2. We send it for birthdays and Christmas.
我們在生日和聖誕節時會寄送
的東西。

4. A fat farm animal with a curly tail.
住在農場裡尾巴捲曲的肥胖動物。

❸ tongue twister
[ˈtʌŋ ˌtwɪstɚ]
繞口令

Eight apes ate eight apples.
八隻猿猴吃了八顆蘋果。

❹ riddle
[ˈrɪdl]
謎語

What has arms
and legs
but can't walk?
什麼東西有手臂和腿
卻不能走路？

A chair.
椅子。

What kind of dog never bites?
什麼種類的狗從不咬人？

A hot dog.
熱狗。

Fortune-telling
[ˈfɔrtʃənˌtɛlɪŋ]

算命

CD2
19

❶ **crystal gazing**
[ˈkrɪstl̩ˌgezɪŋ]
水晶球占卜

❷ **card reading**
[ˈkard ˌridɪŋ]
塔羅牌占卜

❸ **palm reading**
[ˈpam ˌridɪŋ]
看手相

❹ **blood type**
[ˈblʌd ˌtaɪp]
血型

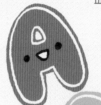
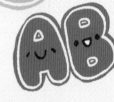

與臺灣和日本相比，英國和美國
較少使用血型來判斷性格。

❺ **fortune cookie**
[ˈfɔrtʃən ˌkʊki]
幸運餅乾

剝開餅乾，會跑出一張籤詩。

At the Amusement Park

[æt] [ði] [əˋmjuzmənt ˏpark]

在遊樂園裡

CD2
20

1 **go-car**
[ˋgoˏkart]
卡丁車

2 **stage**
[stedʒ]
舞臺

3 **popcorn**
[ˋpapˏkɔrn]
爆米花

4 **stand**
[stænd]
攤子

5 **merry-go-round**
[ˋmɛrɪgoˏraʊnd]
旋轉木馬

6 **mascot**
[ˋmæskət]
吉祥物

7 **entrance**
[ˋɛntrəns]
入口

Mom, I want to ride
the roller coaster.

媽媽，我想要玩雲霄飛車。

Mom, I want to take
a picture with the bunny.

媽媽，我想和兔子合照。

8 roller coaster
[ˋrolɚ ͵kostɚ]
雲霄飛車

9 Ferris wheel
[ˋfɛrəs ͵hwil]
摩天輪

10 line
[laɪn]
排隊

12 maze
[mez]
迷宮

11 whirling teacups
[ˋhwɝ·lɪŋ] [ˋti ͵kʌps]
旋轉咖啡杯

14 haunted house
[ˋhɔntɪd] [haʊs]
鬼屋

13 parade
[pəˋred]
遊行

15 souvenir shop
[͵suvəˋnɪr ͵ʃɑp]
紀念品商店

16 clown
[klaʊn]
小丑

Trips

[trɪps]

旅行

CD2 21

瑪娜的興奮海外之旅

❶ departure
[dɪ`partʃɚ]
出發

❷ boarding
[`bordɪŋ]
登機

➡ ➡

出國旅行必備清單

❾ camera
[`kæmərə]
相機

❿ ticket
[`tɪkɪt]
機票

⓫ passport
[`pæs,port]
護照

⓬ money
[`mʌnɪ]
錢

⓭ map
[mæp]
地圖

⓮ souvenir
[,suvə`nɪr]
紀念品

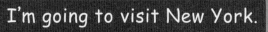

I'm going to visit New York.

我即將去紐約旅行。

Have a nice trip!

祝你旅途愉快！

3 arrival
[əˋraɪvl]
抵達

4 stay
[ste]
停留

5 hotel
[hoˋtɛl]
飯店

8 going home
[goɪŋ] [hom]
回家

7 shopping
[ˋʃɑpɪŋ]
購物

6 sightseeing
[ˋsaɪtˌsiɪŋ]
觀光

TV
[`ti`vi]

電視

CD2
22

What's on TV now?
電視正在播放什麼？

A cooking program.
一個料理節目。

⑩ **TV program** 電視節目
[`ti`vi ˌprogræm]

⑪ **quiz show**
[`kwɪz ˌʃo]
益智節目

⑫ **news program**
[`njuz ˌprogræm]
新聞

⑬ **cartoons**
[kar`tunz]
卡通

❶ power switch
[ˋpaʊɚ ˏswɪtʃ]
電源開關

❷ channel selector
[ˋtʃænl səˏlɛktɚ]
頻道選擇器

❸ volume button
[ˋvaljəm ˏbʌtn̩]
音量按鈕

❹ screen
[skrin]
螢幕

❺ DVD recorder
[ˏdiˏviˋdi rɪˏkɔrdɚ]
DVD燒錄機

❻ remote control
[rɪˋmot kənˋtrol]
遙控

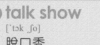

❼ watch TV
[watʃ] [ˋtiˋvi]
看電視

❽ turn on the TV
[ˏtɝn ˋan] [ðə] [ˋtiˋvi]
開電視

❾ turn off the TV
[ˏtɝn ˋɔf] [ðə] [ˋtiˋvi]
關電視

❶❺ talk show
[ˋtɔk ˏʃo]
脫口秀

❶❼ TV commercial
[ˋtiˏvi kəˏmɝˏʃəl]
電視廣告

documentary
[ˏdakjəˋmɛntərɪ]
紀錄片

❶❻ sportscast
[ˋsportsˏkæst]
體育節目

Video Games

[ˋvɪdɪo ˏgemz]

電玩遊戲

CD2
23

> ## Do you know how to play this game?
> 你知道這個遊戲怎麼玩嗎？

3 game console
[ˋgem ˏkɑnsol]
遊戲機

5 role-playing game
[ˋrol ˏpleɪŋ ˏgem]
角色扮演遊戲

▶ 使用攻擊道具

怪物出現了！▾

6 action game
[ˋækʃən ˏgem]
動作遊戲

7 puzzle game
[ˋpʌzl ˏgem]
益智遊戲

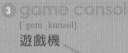

win the game
[wɪn] [ðə] [gem]
遊戲獲勝

② lose the game
[luz] [ðə] [gem]
遊戲落敗

Yes. I completed it.

知道，我已經完成所有關卡了。

④ video game software
[ˋvɪdɪo ˏgem] [ˋsɔft ˏwɛr]
電玩遊戲軟體

racing game
[ˋresɪŋ ˏgem]
競速遊戲

⑨ board game
[ˋbord ˏgem]
圖版遊戲

⑩ shooting game
[ˋʃutɪŋ ˏgem]
射擊遊戲

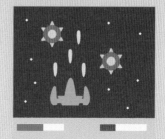

Computers
[kəmˋpjutɚz]

電腦

CD2
24

Let's use the Internet.

來使用網路吧！

1 laptop
[ˋlæptɑp]
筆記型電腦

2 tablet computer
[ˋtæblɪt kəmˏpjutɚ]
平板電腦

3 start the computer
[stɑrt] [ðə] [kəmˋpjutɚ]
開機

5 click
[klɪk]
點擊

4 shut down the computer
[ʃʌt ˋdaʊn] [ðə] [kəmˋpjutɚ]
關機

6 e-mail address
[`imel ˌædrɛs]
電子郵件地址
aaa-xxx@xxxx…

7 e-mail
[`imel]
電子郵件

8 Internet
[`ɪntɚˌnɛt]
網路

10 screen
[skrin]
螢幕

9 website
[`wɛbˌsaɪt]
網站

13 power switch
[`paʊɚ ˌswɪtʃ]
電源開關

11 keyboard
[`kiˌbord]
鍵盤

12 mouse
[maʊs]
滑鼠

14 search
[sɝtʃ]
搜尋

Search

17 password
[`pæsˌwɝd]
密碼

ID

PASS

記住我的密碼

登 入

18 log on
[ˌlɔg `ɑn]
登入

19 log off
[ˌlɔg `ɔf]
登出

15 send an e-mail
[sɛnd] [æn] [`imel]
寄送電子郵件

16 receive an e-mail
[rɪ`siv] [æn] [`imel]
接收電子郵件

20 download
[`daʊnˌlod]
下載

Sports 1
[spɔrts] [wʌn]

運動 1

CD2
25

① soccer
[`sakə]
足球

② goal
[gol]
球門、終點、得分

③ goalkeeper
[`gol͵kipə]
守門員

④ referee
[͵rɛfə`ri]
裁判

10

⑫ swimming
[`swɪmɪŋ]
游泳

⑬ crawl
[krɔl]
自由式

Sports 2
[spɔrts] [tu]

運動 2

CD2
26

❶ gymnastics
[dʒɪmˈnæstɪks]
體操

> **Let's get some exercise.**
> 來做些運動吧！

> **Yes, let's.**
> 好的，來吧！

❷ (American) football
([əˈmɛrɪkən]) [ˈfʊt͵bɔl]
（美式）足球

❸ basketball
[ˈbæskɪt͵bɔl]
籃球

❹ tennis
[ˈtɛnɪs]
網球

❻ badminton
[ˈbædmɪntən]
羽球

❺ volleyball
[ˈvɑlɪ͵bɔl]
排球

8 table tennis
[ˋtebḷ ˏtɛnɪs]
桌球

7 ice hockey
[ˋaɪs ˏhɑkɪ]
冰上曲棍球

9 softball
[ˋsɔft ˏbɔl]
壘球

10 golf 高爾夫球
[gɑlf]

11 rugby （英式）橄欖球
[ˋrʌgbɪ]

12 boxing
[ˋbɑksɪŋ]
拳擊

13 track and field
[ˋtræk ən(d) ˋfild]
田徑

4 horseback riding
[ˋhɔrsˏbæk ˏraɪdɪŋ]
騎馬

15 ballet
[bæˋle]
芭蕾

16 surfing
[ˋsɝfɪŋ]
衝浪

7 skiing
[skiɪŋ]
滑雪

19 wrestling
[ˋrɛslɪŋ]
摔角

18 ice skating
[ˋaɪs ˏsketɪŋ]
溜冰

153

與運動相關的單字

CD2
27

介紹描述運動動作的單字。

❶ play
[ple]
進行（運動）、
打或踢（球）

❷ run
[rʌn]
跑

❸ throw
[θro]
投、擲、拋

❹ hit
[hɪt]
打、擊

❺ catch
[kætʃ]
接

❻ kick
[kɪk]
踢

❼ pass
[pæs]
傳遞

❽ shoot
[ʃut]
射

❾ dribble
[`drɪbl]
運球

❿ attack
[ə`tæk]
進攻

⓫ defend
[dɪ`fɛnd]
防守

⓬ swim
[swɪm]
游

EVENTS

[ɪˋvents]

事件

Months

[mʌnθs]

月

CD2
28

① **season**
[`sizṇ]
季節

⑥ **January**
[`dʒænjʊˌɛrɪ]
一月

⑦ **February**
[`fɛbrʊˌɛrɪ]
二月

⑧ **March**
[martʃ]
三月

⑨ **April**
[`eprəl]
四月

⑩ **May**
[me]
五月

⑪ **June**
[dʒun]
六月

㉖ **weekday**
[`wikˌde]
平日

⑲ **Monday**
[`mʌnde]
星期一

⑳ **Tuesday**
[`tjuzde]
星期二

⑱ **a week**
[ə] [wik]
一星期

㉑ **Wednesday**
[`wɛnzde]
星期三

㉒ **Thursday**
[`θɝzde]
星期四

㉓ **Friday**
[`fraɪde]
星期五

㉗ **weekend**
[`wikˌɛnd]
週末

㉔ **Saturday**
[`sætɚde]
星期六

㉕ **Sunday**
[`sʌnde]
星期日

④ **fall / autumn**
[fɔl] / [ˋɔtəm]
秋

⑤ **winter**
[ˋwɪntɚ]
冬

③ **summer**
[ˋsʌmɚ]
夏

② **spring**
[sprɪŋ]
春

⑫ **July**
[dʒuˋlaɪ]
七月

⑬ **August**
[ˋɔgəst]
八月

⑭ **September**
[sɛpˋtɛmbɚ]
九月

⑮ **October**
[akˋtobɚ]
十月

⑯ **November**
[noˋvɛmbɚ]
十一月

⑰ **December**
[dɪˋsɛmbɚ]
十二月

What's the date today?
今天是幾月幾日？

What day is it today?
今天是星期幾？

It's July 7th.
是7月7日。

It's Friday.
是星期五。

157

Holidays 1

[ˋhɑləˏdez] [wʌn]

節日1

CD2 29

Happy New Year!

新年快樂！

Same to you.

你也是。

❶ New Year's Day
[ˋnju jɪrz ˏde]
元旦
January 1st 1月1日
[ˋdʒænjʊ ˏɛrɪ] [fɝst]

在美國，很多人會在元旦這天，用電視收看足球比賽。

❷ Saint Valentine('s) Day
[sent ˋvæləntaɪnz ˏde]
情人節
February 14th 2月14日
[ˋfɛbrʊ ˏɛrɪ] [ˏfor`tinθ]

Happy Valentine('s) Day!

情人節快樂！

❸ Easter
[ˋistɚ]
復活節

3月21日之後滿月的第一個星期日

這是在春天慶祝耶穌復活的日子。據說復活節兔子會送來彩蛋。

Happy Easter!

復活節快樂！

❺ bunny
[ˋbʌnɪ]
兔子

❹ Easter egg
[ˋistɚ ˏɛg]
復活節彩蛋

6 April Fools' Day
[`eprəl fulz ˌde]
愚人節
April 1st   4月1日
[`eprəl] [fɝst]

這是可以捉弄別人的日子。

Thank you, Mom.

謝謝您，媽媽。

7 Mother's Day
[`mʌðɚz ˌde]
母親節

5月的第二個星期日

Thank you, Dad.

謝謝您，爸爸。

8 Father's Day
[`faðɚz ˌde]
父親節

8月8日（臺灣）

美國、加拿大、日本等
多數國家為6月的第三
個星期日。

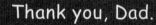

Holidays 2
[ˋhaləˌdez] [tu]

節日2

CD2 30

1 Halloween
[ˌhæloˋin]
萬聖夜（萬聖節前夕）

October 31st
[akˋtobɚ] [ˋθɝtɪ] [fɝst]
10月31日

孩子們會在這天變裝，到鄰居家討糖果。

2 bat
[bæt]
蝙蝠

Happy Halloween!

萬聖夜快樂！

Trick or treat!

不給糖就搗蛋！

3 ghost
[gost]
鬼

4 jack-o'-lantern
[ˋdʒæk ə ˌlæntɚn]
南瓜燈

8 Christmas Day
[ˌkrɪsməs ˋde]
聖誕節

December 25th
[dɪˋsɛmbɚ] [ˋtwɛntɪ] [fɪfθ]
12月25日

慶祝耶穌誕生的日子。
將禮物放在聖誕樹下，在平安夜
或聖誕節當天打開。

9 reindeer
[ˋrenˌdir]
馴鹿

10 holly
[ˋhɑlɪ]
冬青

12 Santa Claus
[ˋsæntə ˌklɔz]
聖誕老人

11 wreath
[riθ]
花環

感謝秋天豐收的日子。
大家會在這一天吃火雞和南瓜派。
加拿大的感恩節在 10 月的第二個星期一。

6 pumpkin pie
[ˋpʌmpkɪn] [paɪ]
南瓜派

7 turkey
[ˋtɝkɪ]
火雞

5 Thanksgiving Day
[ˌθæŋksˋgɪvɪŋ ˌde]
感恩節

11月第四個星期四

15 Christmas tree
[ˋkrɪsməs ˌtri]
聖誕樹

14 light bulb
[ˋlaɪt ˌbʌlb]
燈泡

16 ornament
[ˋɔrnəmənt]
裝飾品

13 bell
[bɛl]
鈴

Merry Christmas!
聖誕節快樂!

School Events

[`skul] [ı`vɛnts]

學校行事

CD2
31

❶ entrance ceremony
[`ɛntrəns] [`sɛrə‚monı]
入學儀式

❷ field trip
[`fild ‚trıp]
遠足、校外教學

I'm in the 100-meter dash toda[y]

我今天要參加 100 公尺賽跑。

I'm cheering for you.

我會為你加油。

❸ field day
[`fild ‚de]
運動會、
校外教學日

FINISH

❹ parents' day
[`pɛrənts ‚de]
家長日

❺ school trip
[`skul ‚trıp]
校外教學

⑥ school festival
[`skul] [`fɛstəvl]
校慶

⑦ spring vacation
[`sprɪŋ] [veˋkeʃən]
春假

⑧ summer vacation
[`sʌmɚ] [veˋkeʃən]
暑假

⑩ graduation
[͵grædʒʊˋeʃən]
畢業、
畢業典禮

⑨ winter vacation
[`wɪntɚ] [veˋkeʃən]
寒假

 各國新學期的開學日和暑假長度不太一樣，例如：臺灣通
常在8月底或9月初展開新學期，暑假大約兩個月；日本
則是在4月展開新學期，暑假一個多月左右。

Parties

[ˋpɑrtɪz]

派對

CD2 32

♪♫ Ken's Birthday Party

① birthday party
[ˋbɝθ,de ,pɑrtɪ]
生日派對

② streamer
[ˋstrimɚ]
飄帶、橫幅

③ balloon
[bəˋlun]
氣球

Happy birthday!
生日快樂！

④ feast
[fist]
宴會

5 invitation card
[ˌɪnvəˈteʃən ˌkard]
邀請函

6 Dear Ann,
Please come to my birthday party.
親愛的安，誠摯邀請您來參加我的生日派對。

◎ Date ◎ May 20, 2017 ※1
◎ Place ◎ my house
◎ Time ◎ 10:30 - 12:30 ※2

日期：2017年5月20日
地點：我的家
時間：10:30～12:30

From Ken 肯 敬邀

7 Dear Ken,
親愛的肯，
Happy birthday to you.
祝你生日快樂。
Your best friend,
Ann
你最好的朋友
安 敬上

8 birthday card
[ˈbɝθ͵de ͵kard]
生日卡片

Make a wish!

許願！

9 candle
[ˈkændl̩]
蠟燭

11 present
[ˈprɛznt]
禮物

10 cake
[kek]
蛋糕

※1 2017年的英語讀作 [tu] [ˈθaʊzn̩d] [͵sɛvənˈtin] 或 [ˈtwɛntɪ] [͵sɛvənˈtin]。
※2 10:30～12:30的英語讀作 [tɛn] [ˈθɝ͵ti] [tɔ] [twɛlv] [ˈθɝ͵ti]。

與臺灣節日相關的單字

CD2
33

介紹臺灣年度活動、節慶和假日的英語表達方式。

❶ New Year's Day
[`nju jɪrz ˌde]
元旦（1月1日）

❷ Chinese New Year
[`tʃaɪniz `nju jɪr]
農曆新年（農曆1月1日）

❸ Lantern Festival
[`læntən] [`fɛstəvl]
元宵節（農曆1月15日）

❹ Children's Day
[`tʃɪldrənz ˌde]
兒童節（4月4日）

❺ Tomb Sweeping Day
[`tum swipɪŋ ˌde]
清明節（日期依農曆清明節氣
而定，通常在國曆4月5日）

❻ Dragon Boat Festival
[`drægən ˌbot] [`fɛstəvl]
端午節（農曆5月5日）

❼ Ghost Festival
[gost] [`fɛstəvl]
中元節（農曆7月15日）

❽ Moon Festival (Mid-Autumn Festival)
[mun] [`fɛstəvl] / [mɪd `ɔtəm] [`fɛstəvl]
中秋節（農曆8月15日）

❾ Teachers' Day
[`titʃəz ˌde]
教師節（9月28日）

❿ Double Tenth Day
[`dʌb tɛnθ ˌde]
雙十節（10月10日）

⓫ Constitution Day
[ˌkɑnstə `tjuʃən ˌde]
行憲紀念日（12月25日）

⓬ Winter Solstice
[`wɪntə] [`salstɪs]
冬至（日期依農曆冬至節氣而定）

LIFE
[laɪf]

生活

Health

[hɛlθ]

健康

CD2 34

How are you feeling today?
你今天感覺如何？

❶ I feel sick.
[aɪ] [fil] [sɪk]
我覺得噁心想吐。

❷ I have a headache.
[aɪ] [hæv] [ə] [`hɛd͵ek]
我覺得頭痛。

❸ I have a stomachache.
[aɪ] [hæv] [ə] [`stʌmək͵ek]
我肚子痛。

❹ I have a sore throat.
[aɪ] [hæv] [ə] [`sor ͵θrot]
我喉嚨痛。

❺ I have a pain here.
[aɪ] [hæv] [ə] [pen] [hɪr]
我覺得這裡疼痛。

❻ I have a cold.
[aɪ] [hæv] [ə] [kold]
我感冒了。

❼ I have a cough.
[aɪ] [hæv] [ə] [kɔf]
我咳嗽。

❽ I have diarrhea.
[aɪ] [hæv] [͵daɪə`riə]
我腹瀉。

❾ I feel itchy here.
[aɪ] [fil] [`ɪtʃɪ] [hɪr]
我覺得這裡很癢。

⑩ I'm fine.
[aɪm] [faɪn]
我很好。

⑪ I have a toothache.
[aɪ] [hæv] [ə] [ˋtuθ‚ek]
我牙齒痛。

⑫ I have a fever.
[aɪ] [hæv] [ə] [ˋfivɚ]
我發燒了。

⑬ I broke my arm.
[aɪ] [brok] [maɪ] [arm]
我的手臂骨折了。

Go to bed.
去睡覺。

Go to the doctor.
去看醫師。

Take some medicine.
吃一些藥。

169

Clothing 1

[ˋkloðɪŋ] [wʌn]

服裝 1

CD2 35

① **collar**
[ˋkɑlɚ]
領子

② **cardigan**
[ˋkɑrdɪgən]
開襟羊毛衫

③ **shorts**
[ʃɔrts]
短褲

④ **dress**
[drɛs]
洋裝

⑤ **sleeve**
[sliv]
袖子

I like your T-shirt

我喜歡你的T恤。

⑩ **pajama**
[pəˋdʒæməs]
睡衣

⑥ **short sleeve**
[ʃɔrt] [sliv]
短袖

⑦ **long sleeve**
[lɔŋ] [sliv]
長袖

⑧ **sweatshirt**
[ˋswɛtˌʃɚt]
長袖運動衣

⑨ **jeans**
[dʒinz]
牛仔褲

⑪ **button**
[ˋbʌtn̩]
鈕釦

170

⑫ **T-shirt**
[ˋti͵ʃɝt]
T恤

⑬ **skirt**
[skɝt]
裙子

⑭ **zipper**
[ˋzɪpɚ]
拉鍊

⑮ **shoes**
[ʃuz]
鞋子

Thank you.

謝謝你。

⑰ **vest**
[vɛst]
背心

⑱ **blouse**
[blaʊz]
（女生的）
上衣、襯衫

⑯ **uniform**
[ˋjunə͵fɔrm]
制服

㉓ **jacket**
[ˋdʒækɪt]
夾克、短外套

⑲ **sweater**
[ˋswɛtɚ]
毛衣

⑳ **coat**
[kot]
外套、大衣

㉑ **pants**
[pænts]
褲子

㉒ **wedding dress**
[ˋwɛdɪŋ ͵drɛs]
婚紗

㉔ **suit**
[sut]
西裝

171

Clothing 2

[`kloðɪŋ] [tu]

服裝2

CD2
36

START

開始

從終點三人的服裝中，推測
三人走的路線分別是什麼？

（答案在254頁）

❶ tights
[taɪts]
緊身褲襪

❷ glasses
[`glæsɪz]
眼鏡

❸ hat
[hæt]
帽子

❹ gloves
[glʌvz]
手套

❺ socks
[saks]
襪子

❻ handkerchief
[`hæŋkɚˌtʃɪf]
手帕

❼ scarf
[skɑrf]
圍巾

❽ boots
[buts]
靴子

❾ mittens
[mɪtnz]
連指手套

❿ slippers
[`slɪpɚz]
拖鞋

⓫ suspenders
[sə`spɛndɚz]
吊帶

⓬ tie
[taɪ]
領帶

13 high heels
[haɪ] [hilz]
高跟鞋

14 scarf
[skarf]
領巾

15 cap
[kæp]
便帽、棒球帽

16 bag
[bæg]
袋子、包包

17 raincoat
[`ren͵kot]
雨衣

18 belt
[bɛlt]
腰帶

19 ribbon
[`rɪbən]
緞帶

20 wallet
[`walɪt]
錢包

21 sneakers
[`snikɚz]
球鞋

22 umbrella
[ʌm`brɛlə]
雨傘

FINISH

終點

Jewelry and Cosmetics

[`dʒuəlrɪ] [ænd] [kaz`mɛtɪks]

珠寶和化妝品

CD2
37

I had my hair cut yesterday.

我昨天剪了頭髮。

❶ **pierced earring**
[pɪrst] [`ɪrɪŋ]
穿耳式耳環

❷ **hair spray**
[`hɛr ˌspre]
髮膠

❸ **lipstick**
[`lɪpˌstɪk]
口紅

❹ **nail polis**
[`nel ˌpalɪʃ]
指甲油

❺ **powder**
[`paʊdə]
（化妝用）粉

❻ **cosmetics**
[kaz`mɛtɪks]
化妝品

174

Looks nice!
看起來不錯！

7 bracelet
[ˋbreslɪt]
手鐲

8 hairpin
[ˋhɛrˌpɪn]
髮夾

9 earring
[ˋɪrɪŋ]
耳環

10 jewel
[ˋdʒuəl]
寶石

11 diamond
[ˋdaɪəmənd]
鑽石

12 ruby
[ˋrubɪ]
紅寶石

13 hair tie
[ˋhɛrˌtaɪ]
髮圈

14 ring
[rɪŋ]
戒指

15 comb
[kom]
梳子

16 perfume
[ˋpɚfjum]、[pɚˋfjum]
香水

17 nail clippers
[nel ˌklɪpɚz]
指甲剪

Jobs 1

[dʒabz] [wʌn]

工作 1

CD2 38

❶ painter
[`pentə]
畫家

❷ politician
[ˌpalə`tɪʃən]
政治家

❸ hairdresser
[`her͵dresə]
美髮師

❹ actor
[`æktə]
演員

❺ cook / chef
[kʊk] / [ʃɛf]
廚師

❻ singer
[`sɪŋə]
歌手

❼ fashion designer
[`fæʃən dɪ͵zaɪnə]
時裝設計師

❽ flight attendant
[`flaɪt ə͵tɛndənt]
空服員

❾ pilot
[`paɪlət]
飛行員

Jobs 2

[dʒabz] [tu]

工作 2

CD2
39

I'm a carpenter.
我是木匠。

What do you do?
你從事什麼工作？

❶ bus driver
[`bʌs ˌdraɪvɚ]
公車司機

❷ announcer
[əˈnaʊnsɚ]
播音員

❸ carpente
[`karpəntɚ]
木匠

❹ tour guide
[`tʊr ˌgaɪd]
導遊

❺ public official
[`pʌblɪk əˈfɪʃəl]
公職人員

❻ teacher
[`titʃɚ]
教師

ABC

❼ nursery school teacher
[`nɝsərɪ skul ˌtitʃɚ]
托兒所或幼兒園老師

❽ police offic
[pəˈlis ˌɔfəsɚ]
警察

9 judge
[dʒʌdʒ]
法官

10 voice actor
[ˋvɔɪs ˌæktɚ]
配音員

11 scientist
[ˋsaɪəntɪst]
科學家

12 doctor
[ˋdɑktɚ]
醫師

13 nurse
[nɝs]
護理師

14 florist
[ˋflɔrɪst]
花匠

15 farmer
[ˋfɑrmɚ]
農夫

16 office worker
[ˋɔfɪs ˌwɝkɚ]
上班族

17 astronaut
[ˋæstrəˌnɔt]
太空人

18 firefighter
[ˋfaɪrˌfaɪtɚ]
消防員

19 vet
[vɛt]
獸醫

Telephone

[ˋtɛləˌfon]

電話

CD2 40

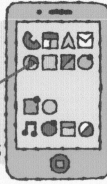

❶ app
[æp]
行動軟體應用程式

❷ smartphone
[ˋsmartˌfon]
智慧型手機

Tell me your cellphone number.
告訴我你的手機號碼。

It's 090-1234-123.
號碼是090-1234-123。

OK.
好的。

Call me tonight.
今晚打電話給我。

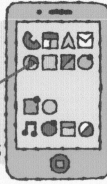

❸ telephone
[ˋtɛləˏfon]
電話

❹ charger
[ˋtʃɑrdʒɚ]
充電器

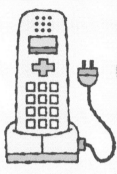

❺ cellphone
[ˋsɛlˏfon]
手機

❻ text message
[ˋtɛkst ˏmɛsɪdʒ]
簡訊

❼ emoticon
[ɪˋmotɪˏkan]
表情符號

早安 ☺
郵件 ♡
謝謝你！

Who's calling, please?

請問您是？

This is Eric.

我是艾瑞克。

Can I speak to Bill?

請問比爾在嗎？

Just a minute, please.

請稍等一下。

181

The World

[ðə] [wɜld]

世界

CD2
41

❶ the world map
[ðə] [ˈwɜld ˌmæp]
世界地圖

❻ the U.K.
[ðə] [ˌjuˈke]
英國

❼ Europe
[ˈjʊrəp]
歐洲

❶5 Russia
[ˈrʌʃə]
俄羅斯

❶6 South Korea
[saʊθ] [kəˈriə]
南韓

❽ France
[fræns]
法國

❾ Germany
[ˈdʒɝməni]
德國

❶7 Asia
[ˈeʃə]
亞洲

❿ Spain
[spen]
西班牙

⓫ Italy
[ˈɪtəli]
義大利

⓬ Egypt
[ˈidʒɪpt]
埃及

❶8 China
[ˈtʃaɪnə]
中國

❶9 India
[ˈɪndɪə]
印度

⓮ Africa
[ˈæfrɪkə]
非洲

⓴ Thailand
[ˈtaɪlænd]
泰國

⓭ the Atlantic Ocean
[ðɪ] [ətˈlæntɪk] [ˈoʃən]
大西洋

㉑ Singapore
[ˈsɪŋɡəˌpor]
新加坡

㉔ Australia
[ɔˈstreljə]
澳大利亞

Where do you want to go?

你想去哪裡？

182

② **north**
[nɔrθ]
北

③ **west**
[wɛst]
西

⑤ **east**
[ist]
東

④ **south**
[saʊθ]
南

㉗ **Canada**
[ˈkænədə]
加拿大

㉘ **North America**
[nɔrθ] [əˈmɛrɪkə]
北美洲

㉒ **Japan**
[dʒəˈpæn]
日本

㉙ **the U.S.A. (America)**
[ðə] [ˌju ɛsˈe] ([əˈmɛrɪkə])
美國

㉓ **the Pacific Ocean**
[ðə] [pəˈsɪfɪk] [ˈoʃən]
太平洋

㉚ **Mexico**
[ˈmɛksɪˌko]
墨西哥

㉕ **Oceania**
[ˌoʃɪˈænɪə]
大洋洲

㉛ **Brazil**
[brəˈzɪl]
巴西

㉖ **New Zealand**
[njuˈzilənd]
紐西蘭

㉜ **South America**
[saʊθ] [əˈmɛrɪkə]
南美洲

I want to go to Germany.
我想去德國。

與世界地圖相關的單字

CD2
42

查看世界地圖時所需的單字。

❶ Northern hemisphere
[`nɔrðən] [`hɛməs‚fɪr]
北半球

❷ Southern hemisphere
[`sʌðən] [`hɛməs‚fɪr]
南半球

❸ equator
[ɪ`kwetə]
赤道

❹ North Pole
[nɔrθ] [pol]
北極

❺ South Pole
[saʊθ] [pol]
南極

❻ line of longitude
[laɪn] [əv] [`lɑndʒə‚tjud]
經線

❼ line of latitude
[laɪn] [əv] [`lætə‚tjud]
緯線

COLORS,

[ˋkʌlɚz]

SHAPES

[ʃeps]

and

[ænd]

NUMBERS

[ˋnʌmbɚz]

顏色、形狀和數字

1   34

5

26   8

Colors

['kʌlɚz]

顏色

1 **deep green**
['dip ,grin]
深綠色

2 **green**
[grin]
綠色

3 **yellow green**
['jɛlo ,grin]
黃綠色

4 **light blue**
['laɪt ,blu]
淺藍色

8 **magenta**
[mə'dʒɛntə]
紫紅色

9 **red**
[rɛd]
紅色

10 **vermilion**
[vɚ'mɪljən]
朱紅色

14 **white**
[hwaɪt]
白色

15 **gray**
[gre]
灰色

16 **brown**
[braʊn]
棕色、褐色

What is your favorite color?
你最喜歡什麼顏色？

It is blue.
藍色。

⑤ blue
[blu]
藍色

⑥ ultramarine
[ˌʌltrəməˈrin]
深藍色

⑦ purple
[ˈpɝpl]
紫色

⑪ orange
[ˈɔrɪndʒ]
橙色

⑫ yellow
[ˈjɛlo]
黃色

⑬ pink
[pɪŋk]
粉紅色

⑰ black
[blæk]
黑色

⑱ gold
[gold]
金色

⑲ silver
[ˈsɪlvɚ]
銀色

Shapes
[ʃeps]

形狀

CD2
44

I like drawing pictures

我喜歡畫圖。

❶ **triangle**
[`traɪˌæŋgl]
三角形

❷ **diamond**
[`daɪəmənd]
菱形

❸ **prism**
[`prɪzm]
角柱體

❹ **cube**
[kjub]
立方體

❺ **cylinder**
[`sɪlɪndə]
圓柱體

❻ **pyramid**
[`pɪrəmɪd]
角錐體

❼ **arrow**
[`æro]
箭頭

❽ **whirl**
[hwɝl]
螺旋形

❾ **sphere**
[sfɪr]
球體

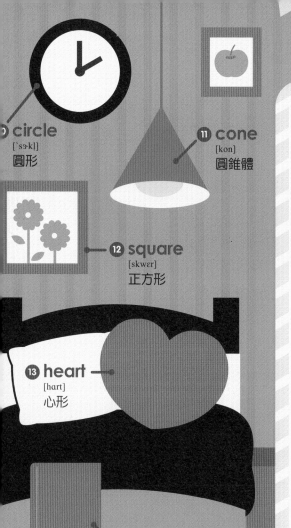

circle
[ˋsɝk!]
圓形

⑪ **cone**
[kon]
圓錐體

⑫ **square**
[skwɛr]
正方形

⑬ **heart**
[hɑrt]
心形

⑭ **rectangle**
[ˋrɛktæŋg!]
長方形

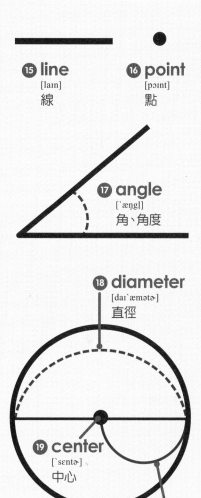

與圖形相關的單字

⑮ **line**
[laɪn]
線

⑯ **point**
[pɔɪnt]
點

⑰ **angle**
[ˋæŋg!]
角、角度

⑱ **diameter**
[daɪˋæmətɚ]
直徑

⑲ **center**
[ˋsɛntɚ]
中心

⑳ **radius**
[ˋredɪəs]
半徑

Numbers 1

[ˋnʌmbɚz] [wʌn]

數字 1

CD2 45

One, two, three four

1、2、3、4……

How many jelly beans are there?

那裡有多少雷根糖？

❶ zero
[ˋzɪro]
0

❷ one
[wʌn]
1

❸ two
[tu]
2

❹ three
[θri]
3

❺ four
[for]
4

❻ five
[faɪv]
5

❼ six
[sɪks]
6

❽ seven
[ˋsɛvən]
7

❾ eight
[et]
8

❿ nine
[naɪn]
9

11 **ten**
[tɛn]
10

12 **eleven**
[ɪˈlɛvən]
11

13 **twelve**
[twɛlv]
12

14 **thirteen**
[ˌθɝˈtin]
13

15 **fourteen**
[ˌforˈtin]
14

16 **fifteen**
[ˌfɪfˈtin]
15

17 **sixteen**
[ˌsɪksˈtin]
16

18 **seventeen**
[ˌsɛvənˈtin]
17

19 **eighteen**
[ˌeˈtin]
18

20 **nineteen**
[ˌnaɪnˈtin]
19

21 **twenty**
[ˈtwɛntɪ]
20

22 **thirty**
[ˈθɝtɪ]
30

23 **forty**
[ˈfɔrtɪ]
40

24 **fifty**
[ˈfɪftɪ]
50

25 **sixty**
[ˈsɪkstɪ]
60

26 **seventy**
[ˈsɛvəntɪ]
70

27 **eighty**
[ˈetɪ]
80

28 **ninety**
[ˈnaɪntɪ]
90

29 **one hundred**
[wʌn] [ˈhʌndrəd]
100

30 **one thousand**
[wʌn] [ˈθaʊzn̩d]
1000

31 **ten thousand**
[tɛn] [ˈθaʊzn̩d]
1萬

32 **one hundred thousand**
[wʌn] [ˈhʌndrəd] [ˈθaʊzn̩d]
10萬

33 **one million**
[wʌn] [ˈmɪljən]
100萬

34 **one hundred million**
[wʌn] [ˈhʌndrəd] [ˈmɪljən]
1億

35 **one billion**
[wʌn] [ˈbɪljən]
10億

Numbers 2

[ˋnʌmbɚz] [tu]

數字2

CD2
46

The mouse cam
in first.

老鼠第一個抵達。

順序的說法

❶ **first**
[fɝst]
第一

❷ **second**
[ˋsɛkənd]
第二

❸ **third**
[θɝd]
第三

次數的說法

How many times
have you been abroad?

你出國幾次？

❽ **once**
[wʌns]
一次

❾ **twice**
[twaɪs]
兩次

❿ **three times**
[θri] [taɪmz]
三次

⓫ **four times**
[fɔr] [taɪmz]
四次

192

The cow came
in second.

牛第二個抵達。

4 fourth
[forθ]
第四

5 fifth
[fɪfθ]
第五

6 twenty-first
[`twɛntɪ] [fɚst]
第二十一

7 hundredth
[`hʌndrədθ]
第一百

分數的說法

12 whole
[hol]
1（全部）

13 a half
[ə] [hæf]
$\frac{1}{2}$

14 a quarter
[ə] [`kwɔrtɚ]
$\frac{1}{4}$

15 a third
[ə] [θɝd]
$\frac{1}{3}$

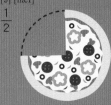

16 three quarters
[θri] [`kwɔrtɚ]
$\frac{3}{4}$

17 two thirds
[tu] [θɝdz]
$\frac{2}{3}$

193

Units

[`junɪts]

單位

CD2 47

About a hundred kilometers.
大約100公里。

How long is this river?
這條河有多長？

長度單位

❶ millimeter
[`mɪlə͵mitɚ]
毫米／公釐（mm）

❷ centimeter
[`sɛntə͵mitɚ]
釐米／公分（cm）

❸ meter
[`mitɚ]
米／公尺（m）

❹ kilometer
[`kɪlə͵mitɚ]
千米／公里（km）

How tall are you?
你身高多高？

I'm 1 meter 22 centimeters tall.
我的身高是122公分。

How heavy is this?
這個東西多重？

It's 2 kilograms.
這個是 2 公斤。

重量單位 **⑤ weight**
[wet]
重量

⑥ gram
[græm]
公克 (g)

⑦ kilogram
[ˋkɪləˏgræm]
公斤 (kg)

⑧ ton
[tʌn]
公噸 (t)

How much milk is left?
剩下多少牛奶？

About 200 milliliters.
大約 200 毫升。

容量單位 **⑨ capacity**
[kəˋpæsətɪ]
容量

⑩ milliliter
[ˋmɪlɪˏlitɚ]
毫升 (ml)

⑪ deciliter
[ˋdɛsəˏlitɚ]
分升／公合 (dl)

⑫ liter
[ˋlitɚ]
公升 (l)

What is the temperature?
溫度幾度？

It's 30 degrees Celsius.
攝氏 30 度。

溫度、角度單位

⑭ temperature
[ˋtɛmprətʃɚ]
溫度

⑮ angle
[ˋæŋgl]
角度、角

⑬ degree
[dɪˋgri]
度

Quantities
[ˈkwantətɪz]

數量

CD2
48

> ## I had a glass of milk this morning.
> 今天早上我喝了一杯牛奶。

1 a slice of bread
[ə] [slaɪs] [əv] [brɛd]
一片麵包

3 a bar of chocolate
[ə] [bɑr] [əv] [ˈtʃɑkəlɪt]
一條巧克力

4 a bottle of water
[ə] [bɑtl] [əv] [ˈwɔtɚ]
一瓶水

2 a can of soda
[ə] [kæn] [əv] [ˈsodə]
一罐汽水

6 a sheet of paper
[ə] [ʃit] [əv] [ˈpepɚ]
一張紙

5 a box of matches
[ə] [baks] [əv] [ˈmætʃɪz]
一盒火柴

7 a jar of jam
[ə] [dʒɑr] [əv] [dʒæm]
一瓶果醬

I had four pieces of cake.

我吃了四塊蛋糕。

8 **a bag of chips**
[ə] [bæg] [əv] [tʃɪps]
一包洋芋片

9 **a piece of cake**
[ə] [pis] [əv] [kek]
一塊蛋糕

10 **a cup of coffee**
[ə] [kʌp] [əv] [ˋkɔfɪ]
一杯咖啡

11 **a pair of pants**
[ə] [pɛr] [əv] [pænts]
一條褲子

13 **a roll of toilet paper**
[ə] [rol] [əv] [ˋtɔɪlɪt ˏpepɚ]
一卷衛生紙

12 **a carton of milk**
[ə] [kɑrtn] [əv] [mɪlk]
一盒牛奶

15 **a pair of shoes**
[ə] [pɛr] [əv] [ʃuz]
一雙鞋

14 **a glass of milk**
[ə] [glæs] [əv] [mɪlk]
一杯牛奶

Time

[taɪm]

時間

CD2
49

〈整點的表達方式〉

What time is it (now)?
（現在）幾點了？

〈現在是 1 點幾分？〉

It's ten (o'clock).
10 點鐘了。

❸ **one-oh-five**
[wʌn] [o] [faɪv]
1:05

It's eleven (o'clock).
11 點鐘了。

❻ **one thirty**
[wʌn] [ˋθɝ·tɪ]
1:30

It's twelve (o'clock).
12 點鐘了。

I need to be home by twelve (o'clock).
我必須在 12 點前到家。

❶ clock
[klɑk]
時鐘

❷ wristwatch
[ˈrɪstˌwɑtʃ]
手錶

❾ one second
[wʌn] [ˈsɛkənd]
1 秒鐘

❿ one minute
[wʌn] [ˈmɪnɪt]
1 分鐘

⓫ one hour
[wʌn] [aʊr]
1 小時

⓬ one day
[wʌn] [de]
1 天

⓭ one week
[wʌn] [wik]
1 星期

⓮ one month
[wʌn] [ˈmʌnθ]
1 個月

⓯ one year
[wʌn] [jɪr]
1 年

⓰ one century
[wʌn] [ˈsɛntʃʊrɪ]
1 世紀

❹ one ten
[wʌn] [tɛn]
1:10

❺ one fifteen
[wʌn] [ˌfɪfˈtin]
1:15

one forty-five
[wʌn] [ˈfɔrtɪ] [faɪv]
1:45

❽ one fifty-five
[wʌn] [ˈfɪftɪ] [faɪv]
1:55

⓱ morning
[ˈmɔrnɪŋ]
早上

⓲ afternoon
[ˌæftɚˈnun]
下午

⓳ evening
[ˈivnɪŋ]
傍晚

20 night
[naɪt]
晚上

199

與時日相關的單字

CD2
50

介紹其他與時間相關的表達方式。

❶ yesterday
['jɛstɚde]
昨天

❷ this morning
[ðɪs] ['mɔrnɪŋ]
今天早上

❸ today
[tə'de]
今天

❹ tonight
[tə'naɪt]
今晚

❺ tomorrow
[tə'mɔro]
明天

❻ last week
[læst] [wik]
上個星期

❼ this week
[ðɪs] [wik]
這個星期

❽ next week
[nɛkst] [wik]
下個星期

❾ now
[naʊ]
現在

❿ before lunch
[bɪ'for] [lʌntʃ]
午餐前

⓫ after lunch
[æftɚ] [lʌntʃ]
午餐後

⓬ ten years ago
[tɛn] [jɪrz] [ə'go]
10 年前

ENGLISH

[ˋɪŋglɪʃ]

英語

Stories
[`stɔrɪz]

故事

CD2
51

4 Big Turnip
[bɪg] [`tɝnɪp]
拔蘿蔔

1 The Wizard of Oz
[ðə] [`wɪzəd] [əv] [`ɔz]
綠野仙蹤

5 Aladdin and His Lamp
[ə`lædn] [ænd] [hɪz] [læmp]
阿拉丁與神燈

6 genie
[`dʒinɪ]
精靈

2 tornado
[tɔr`nedo]
龍捲風

Goodbye, Prince.

再見了，王子。

7 magic lamp
[`mædʒɪk `læmp]
神燈

8 Alice in Wonderland
[`ælɪs] [ɪn] [`wʌndə‚lænd]
愛麗絲夢遊仙境

3 Little Mermaid
[`lɪtl] [`mɝ‚med]
小美人魚

202

9 Snow White and the Seven Dwarfs 白雪公主與七矮人
[sno] [hwaɪt] [ænd] [ðə] [`sɛvən] [dwɔrfs]

10 **apple** 蘋果
[`æpl]

11 **princess**
[`prɪnsəs]
公主

13 **prince**
[prɪns]
王子

12 **Cinderella**
[ˌsɪndə`rɛlə]
仙杜瑞拉

Help!
救命！

14 **coach**
[kotʃ]
馬車

15 **The Wolf and the Seven Kids**
[ðə] [wʊlf] [ænd] [ðə] [`sɛvən] [kɪdz]
狼與七隻小羊

16 **Little Red Riding Hood**
[`lɪtḷ] [rɛd] [`raɪdɪŋ ˌhʊd]
小紅帽

18 **Peter Pan**
[`pitɚ] [pæn]
彼得潘

17 **wolf**
[wʊlf]
狼

19 **pirate**
[`paɪrət]
海盜

203

Opposites 1
[ˋɑpəzɪts] [wʌn]

反義詞 1

CD2 52

❶ strong
[strɔŋ]
強壯的

❷ weak
[wik]
瘦弱的

❹ tall
[tɔl]
高的

❸ short
[ʃɔrt]
矮的

❺ thick
[θɪk]
厚的

❻ thin
[θɪn]
薄的

❼ long
[lɔŋ]
長的

❽ short
[ʃɔrt]
短的

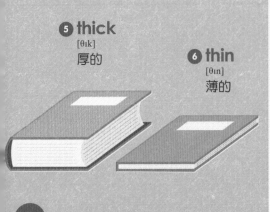

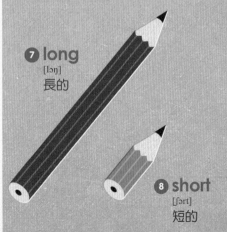

❾ full
[fʊl]
滿的

❿ empty
[ˋɛmptɪ]
空的

⓬ beautiful
[ˋbjutəfəl]
美的

⓫ ugly
[ˋʌglɪ]
醜的

⓮ old
[old]
年長的

⓯ old
[old]
舊的

⓭ young
[jʌŋ]
年輕的

⓰ new
[nju]
新的

⓱ fast / quick
[fæst] / [kwɪk]
快的

⓳ fat
[fæt]
胖的

⓴ thin
[θɪn]
瘦的

⓲ slow
[slo]
慢的

205

Opposites 2
[`apəzɪts] [tu]

反義詞 2

CD2
53

❸ rough
[rʌf]
粗糙的

❹ smooth
[smuð]
平滑的

❷ big
[bɪg]
大的

❶ small
[smɔl]
小的

❻ noisy
[`nɔɪzɪ]
吵鬧的

❺ quiet
[`kwaɪət]
安靜的

❼ hard
[hɑrd]
硬的

❽ soft
[sɔft]
軟的

⑨ bad
[bæd]
壞的

⑩ good
[gʊd]
好的

⑪ light
[laɪt]
輕的

⑫ heavy
[`hɛvɪ]
重的

⑬ open
[`opən]
打開的

⑭ closed
[klozd]
關閉的

⑮ expensive
[ɪk`spɛnsɪv]
貴的

⑯ cheap
[tʃip]
便宜的

$100

SALE

⑰ hot
[hɑt]
炎熱的

⑱ cold
[kold]
寒冷的

⑲ warm
[wɔrm]
溫暖的

⑳ cool
[kul]
涼快的

Opposites 3

[`ɑpəzɪts] [θri]

反義詞 3

CD2
54

1 high
[haɪ]
高的

2 low
[lo]
低的

3 early
[`ɝlɪ]
早的

4 late
[let]
晚的

5 easy
[`izɪ]
簡單的

6 difficult
[`dɪfəˌkəlt]
困難的

7 present
[`prɛzn̩t]
出席的

8 absent
[`æbsənt]
缺席的

208

⑩ far
[fɑr]
遠的

⑨ near
[nɪr]
近的

⑪ careful
[`kɛrfəl]
小心的

⑫ careless
[`kɛrlɪs]
粗心的

⑬ dirty
[`dɝtɪ]
骯髒的

⑭ clean
[klin]
乾淨的

⑮ bright
[braɪt]
亮的

⑯ dark
[dɑrk]
暗的

⑰ rich
[rɪtʃ]
富有的

⑱ poor
[pʊr]
貧窮的

⑲ unlucky
[ʌn`lʌkɪ]
倒楣的

⑳ lucky
[`lʌkɪ]
幸運的

Opposites 4

[ˋɑpəzɪts] [for]

反義詞 4

CD2
55

❶ few
[fju]
少數的

❷ many
[ˋmɛnɪ]
多數的

❸ useful
[ˋjusfəl]
有用的

❹ useless
[ˋjuslɪs]
沒用的

❺ popular
[ˋpɑpjələ]
受歡迎的

❻ unpopular
[ʌnˋpɑpjələ]
不受歡迎的

BAKERY

❼ sharp
[ʃɑrp]
尖銳的

❽ dull
[dʌl]
鈍的

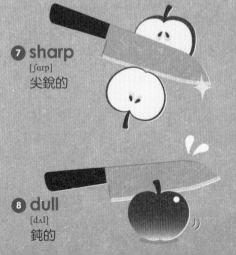

⑨ true
[tru]
真的

⑩ false
[fɔls]
假的

⑪ shallow
[ˋʃælo]
淺的

⑫ deep
[dip]
深的

⑬ wet
[wɛt]
溼的

⑭ dry
[draɪ]
乾的

⑮ little
[ˋlɪtl]
少量的

⑯ much
[mʌtʃ]
大量的

⑰ tight
[taɪt]
緊的

⑱ loose
[lus]
鬆的

⑲ right
[raɪt]
對的

⑳ wrong
[rɔŋ]
錯的

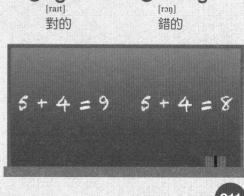

$5 + 4 = 9$ $5 + 4 = 8$

Opposites 5
[`ɑpəzɪts] [faɪv]

反義詞 5

CD2
56

① wake up
[ˌwek `ʌp]
起床

② sleep
[slip]
睡覺

③ begin
[bɪ`gɪn]
開始

④ end
[ɛnd]
結束

THE END

⑤ push
[pʊʃ]
推

⑥ pull
[pʊl]
拉

⑦ teach
[titʃ]
教導

⑧ learn
[lɝn]
學習

9 wide
[waɪd]
寬廣的

10 narrow
[ˋnæro]
狹窄的

11 start
[start]
開始

12 stop
[stap]
停止

14 answer
[ˋænsɚ]
回答

13 ask
[æsk]
詢問

15 succeed
[səkˋsid]
成功

16 fail
[fel]
失敗

17 put on
[ˏpʊt ˋan]
穿上

18 take off
[ˏtek ˋɔf]
脫掉

19 win
[wɪn]
獲勝

20 lose
[luz]
落敗

213

Opposites 6
[`ɑpəzɪts] [sɪks]

反義詞6

CD2
57

❶ give
[gɪv]
給予

❷ receive
[rɪ`siv]
接收

❸ gain
[gen]
獲得

❹ lose
[luz]
失去

❺ forget
[fɚ`gɛt]
遺忘

❻ remember
[rɪ`mɛmbɚ]
記得

❼ sell
[sɛl]
賣

❽ buy
[baɪ]
買

❾ come
[kʌm]
來

❿ go
[go]
去

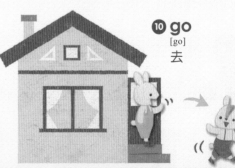

⑪ get on
[ˌgɛt ˋɑn]
上車

⑫ get off
[ˌgɛt ˋɔf]
下車

⑬ send
[sɛnd]
寄送

⑭ receive
[rɪˋsiv]
收到

⑮ stand up
[ˌstænd ˋʌp]
起立

⑯ sit down
[ˌsɪt ˋdaʊn]
坐下

⑰ increase
[ɪnˋkris]
增加

⑱ decrease
[dɪˋkris]
減少

⑲ throw away
[ˌθro əˋwe]
丟掉

⑳ pick up
[ˌpɪk ˋʌp]
拾起

㉑ die
[daɪ]
過世

㉒ live
[lɪv]
活著

215

Opposites 7
[`ɑpəzɪts] [`sɛvən]

反義詞 7

CD2
58

❶ boy
[bɔɪ]
男孩

❸ woman
[`wʊmən]
女人

❹ man
[mæn]
男人

❷ girl
[gɝl]
女孩

❺ front 前面
[frʌnt]

❻ back 後面
[bæk]

❼ success
[sək`sɛs]
成功

❽ failure
[`feljɚ]
失敗

❾ last
[læst]
最後的

❿ first
[fɝst]
第一的

⑪ safety
[`sɛftɪ]
安全

⑫ danger
[`dendʒɚ]
危險

⑬ heaven
[`hɛvən]
天堂

⑭ hell
[hɛl]
地獄

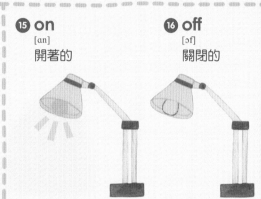

⑮ on
[ɑn]
開著的

⑯ off
[ɔf]
關閉的

⑰ left
[lɛft]
左邊

left
right

⑱ right
[raɪt]
右邊

⑲ up
[ʌp]
向上

⑳ down
[daʊn]
向下

㉑ entrance
[`ɛntrəns]
入口

Haunted House

㉒ exit
[`ɛksɪt]
出口

Locations and Directions
[loˋkeʃənz] [ænd] [dəˋrɛkʃənz]

位置和方向

CD2
59

❶ on the ceiling
[an] [ðə] [ˋsilɪŋ]
在天花板上

❷ in the box
[ɪn] [ðə] [baks]
在盒子裡

❸ behind the box
[bɪˋhaɪnd] [ðə] [baks]
在盒子後面

❹ to the box
[tu] [ðə] [baks]
進去盒子裡

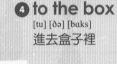

❺ on the table
[an] [ðə] [ˋtebl]
在桌子上面

❼ into the hole
[ˋɪntu] [ðə] [hol]
進去洞穴裡

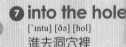

❻ across the street
[əˋkrɔs] [ðə] [strit]
穿過街道

❾ under the table
[ˋʌndɚ] [ðə] [ˋtebl]
在桌子下面

❽ around the chair
[əˋraʊnd] [ðə] [tʃɛr]
在椅子附近

❿ by the plant
[baɪ] [ðə] [plænt]
在植物旁邊

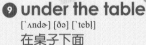

⑪ outside the cage
[ˋaʊtˌsaɪd] [ðə] [kedʒ]
在籠子外面

⑫ above the cat
[əˋbʌv] [ðə] [kæt]
在貓咪上面

⑭ on the wall
[ɑn] [ðə] [wɔl]
在牆上

⑬ inside the cage
[ˋɪnˌsaɪd] [ðə] [kedʒ]
在籠子裡面

Where is the mouse?
老鼠在哪裡？

⑮ near the cat
[nɪr] [ðə] [kæt]
靠近貓咪

⑯ below the cat
[bəˋlo] [ðə] [kæt]
在貓咪下面

⑱ in front of the fireplace
[ɪn] [frʌnt] [əv] [ðə] [ˋfaɪrˌples]
在壁爐前面

⑰ out of the hole
[aʊt] [əv] [ðə] [hol]
在洞穴外面

⑲ at the door
[æt] [ðə] [dor]
在門口

⑳ among the cushions
[əˋmʌŋ] [ðə] [ˋkʊʃənz]
在靠墊之中

㉑ between the cushions
[bɪˋtwin] [ðə] [ˋkʊʃənz]
在靠墊中間（兩者之間）

在驚訝、開心、呼喚、回答等時候所發出的聲音。

⑩ Wow!
哇!

⑪ Oh!
噢!

⑫ Ouch!
哎喲!(疼痛)

⑬ Ahchoo!
哈啾!(噴嚏聲)

⑭ Yummy!
好吃!

⑯ ZZZ.
呼嚕。(鼾聲)

⑮ Boohoo.
哇——(大哭)

Useful Phrases
[ˋjusfəl] [ˋfreziz]

常用片語

CD2
61

❶ Good morning.
早安。

❷ Good afternoon.
午安。

❸ Good evening.
晚上好。

❹ How are you?
你好嗎？

❺ Fine, thank you.
很好，謝謝你。

❻ Hello, Bob.
哈囉，鮑伯。

❼ Hi, Yumi.
嗨，尤美。

❽ Nice to meet you, Ken.
肯，很高興認識你。

大部分會在「Hello」等打招呼的單字後面加上對方的名字。

⑨ Good night.
晚安。

⑬ Goodbye.
再見。

⑭ Bye.
再見。

⑩ Really?
真的嗎？

⑮ Thank you.
謝謝你。

⑯ You're welcome.
別客氣。

⑪ Pardon?
請再說一遍？

⑫ Excuse me.
不好意思。

⑰ I'm sorry.
我很抱歉。

⑱ That's all right.
沒關係。

KK音標表

KK音標由美國語言學家 Kenyon 和 Knott 所編訂，是一套描述英語發音的符號系統。學生除了以自然發音法（或稱自然拼讀法）為學習基礎，亦可使用 KK音標作為輔助，並藉此補足自然發音的例外情況。但無論使用自然發音法或 KK音標，都建議學習新單字時，仔細聆聽 CD、反覆開口練習，更能提升英語發音的實力。

母音音標	字母拼讀舉例
[i]	me, see, tea
[ɪ]	kiss, yummy
[e]	day, rain, eight, they
[ɛ]	egg, pencil
[æ]	apple
[u]	room, you, ruby
[ʊ]	book, pull
[o]	ocean
[ɔ]	off, ball, daughter
[ɑ]	hot, father
[ʌ]	but, money
[ə]	about, elephant, tonight
[ɝ]	girl, surprise
[ɚ]	river, doctor
[aɪ]	die, bye
[aʊ]	how, cloud
[ɔɪ]	joy, voice

子音音標	字母拼讀舉例
[p]	page, sleep
[b]	baby, rub
[d]	day, board
[t]	table, little
[k]	cat, cook
[g]	get, egg
[f]	face, golf, phrase
[v]	vase, wave
[s]	sad, class
[z]	nose, zebra
[θ]	tooth, thin
[ð]	this, father
[ʃ]	ship, wash
[ʒ]	television, garage
[tʃ]	chip, coach
[dʒ]	jam, cage
[h]	hair
[m]	man, ham
[n]	nail, lawn
[ŋ]	spring
[l]	last, college
[r]	rabbit, car
[j]	yard
[w]	win
[(h)w]	whale

中文索引

依照第一個字的筆畫順序排列，指出英語單字所在頁面。

英語索引

依照第一個字母順序排列，指出英語單字所在頁面。

答案

p.68-69

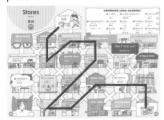

p.136（填字遊戲）

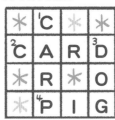

p.114-115

p.172-173

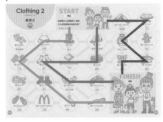

p.120-121

※男生的答案是藍線，小男孩
　的答案是綠線，女生的答案
　是紅線。

製作這本書的人

佐藤久美子

日本玉川大學研究所教育學研究科（教職專攻）教授。畢業於津田塾大學學藝學部英文科，津田塾大學研究所博士課程修畢。曾留學於倫敦大學研究所博士課程，專攻語言心理學及英語教育。

長年致力於研究兒童的聲音語言習得方式、語言發展過程，以及母子相互作用的影響等，並推展以科學理論資料為基礎的英語教育指導法及教材的開發。

於1998年至2002年、2012年至2016年間擔任NHK廣播電臺「基礎英語3」、「基礎英語2」講師。此外，還獲得町田市、國立市、葛飾區、板橋區、京都府等地教育委員會邀請，設計小學英語教育課程及教材，並擔任教師研習講座的講師。

2008年開始擔任J-SHINE（小學英語指導者認定協議會）理事。2012年開始擔任NHK教育頻道「以英語來玩遊戲」、「以英語來玩遊戲with Orton」的綜合指導。2017年開始擔任NHK教育頻道「英語beat」的節目委員。

著有《「小學英語」指導法手冊》（玉川大學出版部編譯）、《今天開始我也要當英語老師！小學英語指導法導覽手冊》（玉川大學出版部共著）、《因為想說，英語語法！》（朝日出版社）、《Welcome to Tokyo: Elementary教師用指導書》（東京都教育委員會）、《立即就能教的小學英語指導案集》（朝日出版社）等。

封面插圖、裝訂 ………… Indy Design 高橋進
內文設計 ………… 富田明日香
英文執筆、校對 …… Steve Lia（玉川大學副教授）、Joseph R.Tabolt
協助編輯 ………… 秋下幸惠、小縣宏行、齋藤友希、佐藤美穗、田中裕子、宮崎史子、渡邊泰葉
內文插畫 ………… 池義明、服部菜美、GyoGyoMaaMa、岩西真由美、caramel mountain、生武誠、堀井惠美、谷口幸一、aque、TOFU、丸尾晶子、富田明日香、今浦咲良、田上奈央子、蔦澤綾子、rikko
地圖製作 ………… Them STUDIO
電腦排版 ………… 四國寫研
聲音收錄 ………… ELEC
旁白配音 ………… Edith Kayumi、Josh Keller、水月優希
企畫、編輯 ……… 高山春花（學研辭典編輯部）

國家圖書館出版品預行編目 (CIP) 資料

NEW 全彩學生快速記憶英語圖鑑字典：情境學習常用單字、片語和會話句型／佐藤久美子監修 .-- 初版 .-- 新北市：小熊，2019.06

272 面；14.8×21 公分 .-- (英語學習)

譯自：新レインボー はじめて英語図鑑 CD つき オールカラー

ISBN 978-957-8640-92-4 (精裝)

1. 英語 2. 字典

805.132　　　　　　　　　　　　　　108007004

英語學習

NEW 全彩學生快速記憶英語圖鑑字典

情境學習常用單字、片語和會話句型

Best English Picture Dictionary for Students

監修：佐藤久美子（日本玉川大學研究所名譽教授・特任教授）

審訂：馮和平（臺灣師範大學英語學系副教授）

總編輯：鄭如瑤｜責任編輯：陳怡潔｜美術編輯：莊芯媚

編輯協助：卓文怡（日文翻譯）、鄭文怡（英語翻譯）｜行銷副理：塗幸儀

錄音：印笛錄音製作有限公司

出版：小熊出版／遠足文化事業股份有限公司

發行：遠足文化事業股份有限公司（讀書共和國出版集團）

地址：231 新北市新店區民權路 108-3 號 6 樓

電話：02-22181417｜傳真：02-86672166

劃撥帳號：19504465｜戶名：遠足文化事業股份有限公司

Facebook：小熊出版｜E-mail：littlebear@bookrep.com.tw

讀書共和國出版集團網路書店：www.bookrep.com.tw

客服專線：0800-221029｜客服信箱：service@bookrep.com.tw

團體訂購請洽業務部：02-22181417 分機 1124

法律顧問：華洋法律事務所／蘇文生律師｜印製：漾格科技股份有限公司

初版一刷：2019 年 6 月｜初版五刷：2020 年 7 月｜初版十刷：2023 年 7 月

定價：650 元｜ISBN：978-957-8640-92-4｜書號：0BEL1001

Shin Rainbow Hajimete Eigo Zukan

© Gakken 2017

First published in Japan 2017 by Gakken Plus Co., Ltd., Tokyo

Traditional Chinese translation rights arranged with Gakken Plus Co., Ltd. through Future View Technology Ltd.

小熊出版官方網頁　　　小熊出版讀者回函

PERSON 人 (1)

（實力UP單字卡，共16張，沿虛線裁下，隨身攜帶，時時複習。）

Body 身體
head 頭
face 臉
neck 脖子
hand 手
arm 手臂
stomach 肚子
navel 肚臍
leg 腿
shoulder 肩膀
chest 胸
armpit 腋下
back 背
waist 腰
buttocks 屁股
foot 腳 (單數)
skull 頭骨
joint 關節
bone 骨頭
skin 皮膚
muscle 肌肉
heart 心臟

lung 肺
brain 腦
vein 血管
blood 血液
internal organs 內臟

Feet 腳
thigh 大腿
knee 膝蓋
shin 脛
calf 小腿肚
leg 腿
instep 腳背
toenail 腳指甲
toe 腳趾
ankle 踝
foot 腳 (單數)
feet 腳 (複數)
heel 腳後跟
sole 腳底
stand 站立
walk 走

run 跑
skip 輕快的跳
jump 跳
hop 單腳跳
sit 坐
kick 踢
stand up 起立
slip 滑
crawl 爬
climb 攀爬

Hands 手
finger 手指
forefinger 食指
middle finger 中指
third finger 無名指
little finger 小指
palm 手掌
thumb 拇指
nail 指甲
hand 手
arm 手臂

elbow 手肘
touch 摸
hold 握
point 指
wave 揮
grab 抓
catch 接
throw 投、擲、拋
press 按
clap 拍
knock 敲
scratch 抓、劃
rub 擦

1

PERSON 人 (3)

Emotions 情緒
happy 快樂的
disappointed 沮喪的
sad 悲傷的
lonely 孤單的
bored 無聊的
surprised 驚訝的
worried 煩惱的
moved 感動的
shocked 震驚的
delighted 高興的
angry 生氣的
satisfied 滿足的
amused 被逗樂的
afraid 害怕的
anxious 焦慮的
nervous 緊張的
annoyed 惱怒的
confused 困惑的

Family 家庭
grandparents 外祖父母
　　/祖父母
grandmother 外祖母/外婆
　　/祖母/奶奶
grandfather 外祖父/外公
　　/祖父/爺爺
uncle 姨丈/舅舅/伯父
　　/叔叔/姑丈
aunt 阿姨/舅媽/伯母
　　/嬸嬸/姑姑
parents 父母
mother 媽媽
father 爸爸
cousin 表 (或堂) 兄弟姊妹
sister 姊姊/妹妹
I/ me 我
brother 哥哥/弟弟

其他
child 孩子 (單數)
children 孩子 (複數)
son 兒子
daughter 女兒
baby 嬰兒
niece 外甥女、姪女
nephew 外甥、姪兒
grandchild 孫子、孫女
husband 丈夫
wife 妻子
second cousin 父母的堂 (或
　　表) 兄弟姊妹的子女
relative 親戚

3

PERSON 人 (2)

Face 臉
tongue 舌頭
dimple 酒窩
hair 頭髮
eyebrow 眉毛
ear 耳朵
cheek 臉頰
nose 鼻子
mouth 嘴巴
lip 嘴脣
chin 下巴
forehead 額頭
temple 太陽穴
eyelash 睫毛
eye 眼睛
freckle 雀斑

tooth 牙齒 (單數)
teeth 牙齒 (複數)
mole 痣
throat 喉嚨
watch 觀看
look at 注意看
see 看見
hear 聽
listen to 注意聽
smell 聞
kiss 親
whistle 吹口哨
smile 微笑
laugh 大笑 (笑出聲音)
cry 哭 (哭出聲音)
weep 流淚

Personalities 個性
humorous 幽默的
cheerful 高興的
polite 有禮貌的
smart 聰明的
friendly 友善的
shy 害羞的
brave 勇敢的
careful 仔細的、小心的
strong 強壯的
strict 嚴格的
honest 正直的
kind 親切的
patient 能忍受的、有耐心的
active 活潑的
curious 好奇的

HOUSE 家 (1)

Around the House
住家周遭
second floor 二樓
first floor 一樓
garage 車庫
dining room 飯廳
study 書房
ceiling 天花板
hall 門廳
wall 牆壁
roof 屋頂
attic 閣樓
chimney 煙囪
bedroom 臥房
window 窗戶
stairs 樓梯
floor 地板
living room 客廳
bathroom 浴室
front door 正門
mailbox 郵箱
yard 庭院

fence 圍籬
neighbor 鄰居

In the Living Room
在客廳裡
door 門
switch 開關
curtain 窗簾
sofa 沙發
cushion 靠墊、坐墊
light 燈
air conditioner 空調、冷暖氣機
vase 花瓶
window 窗戶
telephone 電話
clock 時鐘
outlet 插座
picture 圖畫
tissues 面紙
newspaper 報紙
table 桌子
television 電視

remote control 遙控
trash can 垃圾桶
rug 地毯

In the Dining Room
在飯廳裡

salt shaker 鹽罐
pepper shaker 胡椒罐
cup 杯子
plate 盤子
cupboard 櫥櫃
glass 玻璃杯
bottle opener 開瓶器
table 桌子
napkin 餐巾
chopsticks 筷子
bowl 碗
fork 叉子
knife 刀子
spoon 湯匙
chair 椅子
tablecloth 桌巾

HOUSE 家 (2)

In the Kitchen
在廚房裡
kitchen fan 抽油煙機
refrigerator 冰箱
freezer 冷凍庫
frying pan 煎鍋
ladle 杓子
whisk 攪拌器
stove 爐子
pot 鍋子
lid 蓋子
kettle 壺
cutting board 砧板
kitchen knife 菜刀
sink 水槽
dish towel 擦碗布
oven 烤箱
dishwasher 洗碗機
apron 圍裙
microwave oven 微波爐
rice cooker 電鍋
bowl 碗

measuring cup 量杯
measuring spoon 量匙
peeler 削皮器

In the Bathroom
在浴室裡
mirror 鏡子
hand towel 擦手巾
faucet 水龍頭
cabinet 櫃子
hand soap 洗手乳
scale 體重計
sink 水槽
bath mat 浴室地墊
toothbrush 牙刷
toothpaste 牙膏
hairbrush 梳子
hairdryer 吹風機
weigh myself 量體重
wash my face 洗臉
wash my hands 洗手
gargle 漱喉、漱口

brush my teeth 刷牙
rinse my mouth 漱口
brush my hair 梳頭髮
dry my hair 吹頭髮
shower 淋浴設備
bath towel 浴巾
washcloth（擦臉用）毛巾
rinse 潤絲精
shampoo 洗髮精
soap 肥皂
bathtub 浴缸
drain 排水孔
washing bowl 臉盆
bubble 泡泡
toilet paper 衛生紙
toilet 馬桶
wash myself 洗澡
wash my hair 洗頭
take a shower 淋浴
flush the toilet 沖馬桶
go to the bathroom 去洗手間

FOOD 食物 (1)

Fruit 水果
rind （硬的）果皮
flesh 果肉
seed 種子
peel 果皮
shell 果殼
banana 香蕉
pineapple 鳳梨
coconut 椰子
pear 梨
papaya 木瓜
blueberry 藍莓
fig 無花果
avocado 酪梨
kiwi 奇異果
tangerine 橘子、紅橘
orange 柳橙、柑橘
grapefruit 葡萄柚
apple 蘋果
melon 哈密瓜
strawberry 草莓

lemon 檸檬
mango 芒果
persimmon 柿子
cherry 櫻桃
peach 水蜜桃
grapes 葡萄
Japanese pear 白梨
walnut 核桃
chestnut 栗子

Vegetables 蔬菜
turnip 蕪菁
parsley 香芹
mushroom 菇
lettuce 萵苣
cabbage 甘藍
onion 洋蔥
broccoli 青花菜
cauliflower 花椰菜
garlic 大蒜
cucumber 黃瓜

spinach 菠菜
asparagus 蘆筍
potato 馬鈴薯
lotus root 蓮藕
Japanese radish 日本蘿蔔
carrot 紅蘿蔔
pumpkin 南瓜
green pepper 青椒
eggplant 茄子
tomato 番茄
peas 豌豆
leek 韭蔥
Chinese cabbage 大白菜
sweet potato 番薯
celery 芹菜
bean sprouts 豆芽
corn 玉米
burdock 牛蒡

HOUSE 家 (3)

In the Bedroom 在臥房裡
alarm clock 鬧鐘
lamp 燈
dresser 梳妝臺
shelf 架子
drawer 抽屜
closet 衣櫃
pillow 枕頭
sheet 床單
mattress 床墊
blanket 毯子
comforter 棉被
bed 床
desk 書桌
sleep 睡覺
yawn 打呵欠
dream 做夢
wake up 起床
go to bed 就寢
take a nap 打盹
oversleep 睡過頭

In the Yard 在庭院裡
hedge 樹籬
flowerbed 花圃
watering can 灑水壺
soil 泥土
brick 磚塊
shovel 鏟子
hose 水管
fertilizer 肥料
lawn 草坪
bucket 水桶
tree 樹
flowerpot 花盆
hammock 吊床
doghouse 狗屋

Housework 家事
dryer 烘乾機
washing machine 洗衣機
dustpan 畚箕
vacuum cleaner 吸塵器
broom 掃帚
dust 灰塵
dish 碟子、盤子
dish towel 擦碗布
sponge 海綿
laundry basket 洗衣籃
clothespin 晒衣夾
detergent 洗滌劑、洗衣粉
cleaning cloth 抹布
ladder 梯子
hanger 衣架
iron 熨斗
thread 線
needle 針
sewing machine 縫紉機
woolen yarn 毛線
cloth 布

其他
clean 清潔
cook 煮
wash 洗
wipe 擦拭
sweep 清掃
sew 縫紉
knit 編織
bundle 綑綁
squeeze 擰、壓
water the flowers 澆花
weed 除草
mow 割草

6

FOOD 食物 (2)

Meals 餐點
breakfast 早餐
boiled egg 水煮蛋
sausage 香腸
bacon 培根
cereal 麥片
jam 果醬
yogurt 優格
scrambled eggs 炒蛋
toast 烤吐司
lunch 午餐
sandwich 三明治
dinner 晚餐
curry and rice 咖哩飯
rice 米飯
bread 麵包
noodles 麵
egg 蛋
cheese 起司
salad 沙拉
seafood 海鮮
fish 魚

chicken 雞肉
pork 豬肉
beef 牛肉
meat 肉
menu 菜單
hamburger 漢堡
hot dog 熱狗
French fries 薯條
fried chicken 炸雞
chef's recommendations
　主廚推薦
pizza 披薩
soup 湯
gratin 焗烤燉菜
omelet 蛋包飯
steak 牛排
potage 濃湯
spaghetti 義大利麵
beef stew 燉牛肉
sautéed fish 煎魚排
fried prawn 炸蝦
roast beef 烤牛肉

Drinks 飲品
coffee 咖啡
soda pop 汽水
cafe 咖啡廳
lemonade 檸檬汽水
ginger ale 薑汁汽水
orange juice 柳橙汁
cola 可樂
ice cream float
　漂浮冰淇淋
tea 茶
cocoa 可可
green tea 綠茶
alcohol 酒
soy milk 豆漿
milk 牛奶
water 水
cup 杯子
glass 玻璃杯
saucer 茶托
straw 吸管
mug 馬克杯

8

FOOD 食物 (3)

Confectionery 甜點
ice cream 冰淇淋
lollipop 棒棒糖
candy 糖果
jelly bean 雷根糖
chocolate 巧克力
cupcake 杯子蛋糕
cake 蛋糕
apple pie 蘋果派
cheesecake 起司蛋糕
parfait 百匯、凍糕
custard pudding 焦糖布丁
jello 果凍
pancake 鬆餅
donut 甜甜圈
crepe 可麗餅
cracker 薄脆餅乾
cookie 餅乾
popcorn 爆米花
potato chips 洋芋片
mashed sweet potatoes
　番薯泥

Cooking 料理
cut 切
peel 削、剝
slice 切片
chop 切碎
bake 烘烤
grate 磨碎
mash 搗碎成泥
boil 烹煮、煮沸
whip 攪打
stir 攪拌
pour 倒入
stew 燉煮
fry 油煎
roast 烘烤
grill（用烤架）燒烤
deep(-)fry 油炸
toast 烤（麵包）
steam 蒸
freeze 冷凍
sugar 糖
salt 鹽

pepper 胡椒
butter 奶油
flour 麵粉
oil 油
sauce 醬料、醬油
ketchup 番茄醬
vinegar 醋
honey 蜂蜜

其他
eat 吃
bite 咬
chew 咀嚼
lick 舔
drink 喝
bitter 苦的
sweet 甜的
hot 熱的、辣的
spicy 香料多的、辣的
sour 酸的
salty 鹹的
delicious 美味的

9

TOWN 城鎮 (2)

At the Supermarket 在超市裡
beverages 飲料
meat 肉
seafood 海鮮
store clerk 店員
fruit 水果
vegetables 蔬菜
eggs 蛋
dairy products 乳製品
money 錢
bill 帳單
change 找零
coin 硬幣
receipt 收據
checkout counter 收銀臺
checkout bag 購物袋
shopping basket 購物籃
tasting samples 試吃
frozen foods 冷凍食品
bakery 麵包店
canned goods 罐裝食品
shopping cart 購物手推車
pet foods 寵物食品

sale 出售、特賣
cosmetics 化妝品
snacks 零食
candy 糖果
shopping list 購物清單
banana 香蕉
milk 牛奶
ham 火腿
chocolate 巧克力

At the Hospital 在醫院裡
patient 病患
shot 注射
stethoscope 聽診器
(clinical) thermometer 體溫計
nurse 護理師
medicine 藥
medical records 病歷
doctor 醫師
operation 手術
bed 床
X-ray X光
bandage 繃帶

disinfectant 消毒水
adhesive bandage ok繃
compress（消炎等）敷布

At the Park 在公園裡
play on the seesaw 玩翹翹板
seesaw 翹翹板
walk the dog 遛狗
bench 長凳
slide 滑梯
play on the slide 溜滑梯
sandbox 沙坑
horizontal bar 單槓
practice on a horizontal bar
　練習撐單槓
fountain 噴水池
swing on a swing 盪秋千
swing 秋千
pond 池塘
climbing bar 爬桿
statue 雕像
jungle gym 攀爬架

11

TOWN 城鎮 (1)

In the City 在城市裡
shrine 神社
temple 寺廟
department store 百貨公司
apartment 公寓
nursery school 幼兒園、托兒所
school 學校
restaurant 餐廳
movie theater 電影院
library 圖書館
factory 工廠
stadium 體育場
station 車站
office building 辦公大樓
city hall 市政府
post office 郵局
fire station 消防局
hospital 醫院
bank 銀行
police station 警察局
park 公園

hotel 飯店
museum 博物館
church 教堂

Stores 商店
shopping list 購物清單
T-shirt T恤
cold medicine 感冒藥
chicken 雞肉
candy 糖果
rose 玫瑰
battery 電池
tuna 鮪魚
book 書
roll 麵包卷
pencil 鉛筆
tomato 番茄
glasses shop 眼鏡行
clothing store 服飾店
vegetable store 蔬菜店
sporting goods store 運動用品店

bookstore 書店
jewelry shop 珠寶店
cleaner's 洗衣店
toy store 玩具店
candy store 糖果店
pet shop 寵物店
fish shop 魚鋪
drugstore 藥局
electronics store 電器行
convenience store 便利商店
stationery store 文具店
cafe 咖啡廳
liquor store 酒館
flower shop 花店
bakery 麵包店
butcher shop 肉鋪
shoe store 鞋店
beauty salon 美容院

TOWN 城鎮 (3)

Roads 道路
slope 斜坡
traffic accident 交通事故
sign 交通號誌
dead end 死路
tactile paving 導盲磚
parking lot 停車場
gas station 加油站
traffic light 交通號誌燈
manhole（下水道等供人出入的）人孔
mailbox 郵筒
railroad crossing 鐵路平交道
crosswalk 行人穿越道
street 街道
expressway 高速公路
sidewalk 人行道
signboard 看板
intersection 十字路口
street light 路燈
bridge 橋梁

shortcut 捷徑
corner 轉角
tunnel 隧道
traffic jam 塞車
bus stop 公車停靠站
pedestrian overpass 天橋

Cars and Bicycles
汽車和腳踏車
unicycle 單輪車
tricycle 三輪車
car 汽車
GPS 全球衛星定位系統
steering wheel 方向盤
horn 喇叭
accelerator 油門
brake 煞車
passenger's seat 副駕駛座
parking brake 手煞車
driver's seat 駕駛座
door 門

driver 駕駛
wiper 雨刷
seat belt 安全帶
turn signal 方向燈
head light（車）頭燈
license plate 車牌
tire 輪胎
bicycle/ bike 腳踏車
helmet 安全帽
training wheels 輔助輪
chain 鍊子
pedal 腳踏板
saddle 坐墊
brake 煞車
handlebars（腳踏車的）手把
air pump 打氣筒

TOWN 城鎮 (4)

At the Station 在車站裡
elevator 電梯
driver 駕駛
train 火車
strap 拉環
escalator 電扶梯
priority seat 博愛座
passenger 乘客
seat 座位
door 門
route map 路線圖
timetable 時刻表
track 軌道
ticket 票、券
smart card IC卡
platform 月臺
ticket gate 票閘
information 服務臺
fare table 票價表
ticket machine 售票機
coin-operated locker 投幣式
　置物櫃

Transportation 交通工具
flying carpet 魔毯
ship 船
hot air balloon 熱氣球
sailboat 帆船
tanker 油罐車
monorail 單軌列車
truck 卡車
motorcycle 機車
dump truck 自卸卡車
ambulance 救護車
bus 公車
police car 警車
taxi 計程車
airplane/ plane 飛機
helicopter 直升機
bicycle/ bike 腳踏車
parachute 降落傘
fire engine 消防車
boat 小船
wheelchair 輪椅
car 汽車

bullet train 高速火車
subway 地鐵
train 火車
baby carriage 嬰兒車
cable car 纜車

其他
buy a ticket 購票
get on a train 上火車
get off a train 下火車
wait for the train 等火車
change trains 轉乘火車
drive a car 開車（汽車）
get into a car 上車（汽車）
get out of a car 下車（汽車）
park a car 停車（汽車）
ride a bicycle 騎腳踏車
speed up 加速
slow down 減速

⑬

SCHOOL 學校 (2)

In the Classroom
在教室裡
speaker 擴音機
blackboard 黑板
shelf 架子
homeroom teacher
　班級導師
chalk board eraser 板擦
chalk 粉筆
goal 目標
thumbtack 圖釘
handout 講義
chair 椅子
desk 書桌
classmate 同學
indoor shoes 室內鞋
textbook 教科書
schoolbag 書包
drawer 抽屜

School Supplies
學用品
protractor 量角器
triangle 三角板
report card 成績單
journal 日記
calculator 計算機
box cutter 美工刀
packing tape 封箱膠帶
Scotch tape 透明膠帶
abacus 算盤
compasses 圓規
stapler 訂書機
sticker 貼紙
notebook 筆記本
pencil case 鉛筆盒
globe 地球儀
paper clip 迴紋針
pencil 鉛筆
eraser 橡皮擦
ballpoint pen 原子筆
scissors 剪刀

colored pencil 色鉛筆
glue 膠水
crayon 蠟筆
paint 顏料
pencil sharpener 削鉛
　筆機
paint（用繪圖工具）繪畫
draw（畫圖或線條）繪畫
write 書寫
erase 擦掉
paste 黏
stick on 貼
cut 剪

In the Science Room
在自然科學教室裡
miniature bulb 小燈泡
dry battery 乾電池
astronomical telescope
　天文望遠鏡
beaker 燒杯

flask 燒瓶
dropper 滴管
liquid 液體
flame 火焰
thermometer 溫度計
gas burner 氣體燃燒器
magnifying glass 放大鏡
microscope 顯微鏡
powder 粉末
tweezers 鑷子
magnet 磁鐵
test tube 試管
experiment 實驗
observe 觀察
discover 發現

⑮

SCHOOL 學校 (1)

School 學校
preschool 幼兒園
kindergarten 幼兒園
elementary school 小學
junior high school 國中
high school 高中
college 大學
vocational school 職業學校
junior college 專科學校
first grade 一年級
second grade 二年級
third grade 三年級
fourth grade 四年級
fifth grade 五年級
sixth grade 六年級
enter 進入（入學）
graduate 畢業
diploma 畢業證書
yearbook 畢業紀念冊

School Rooms 校舍
gym 體育館
schoolyard 校園
swimming pool 游泳池
school gate 校門
library 圖書館
music room 音樂教室
science room 自然科學教室
nurse's room 保健室
computer room 電腦教室
art room 美術教室
teacher 老師
classroom 教室
student 學生
entrance 入口
office 辦公室
teacher's room 教師辦公室
principal 校長
vice-principal 副校長
restroom 洗手間

School Subjects 學習科目
go to school 上學
attend class 上課
take a test 考試
have school lunch 吃營養午餐
Mandarin 國語
Mathematics 數學
Natural Sciences 自然科學
Social Studies 社會
English 英語
Civics and Society 公民與社會
Arts 藝術
Health and Physical
    Education 健康與體育
Geography 地理
Integrative Activities 綜合活動
Midday (Rest) Break 午休時間
Technology 科技
Calligraphy 書法
History 歷史
Class Meeting 班會
Club Activities 社團活動
go home 回家

14

SCHOOL 學校 (3)

In the Music Room
在音樂教室裡
cymbals 鈸
piano 鋼琴
chorus 合唱、合唱團
tambourine 鈴鼓
castanets 響板
accordion 手風琴
harmonica 口琴
recorder 直笛
conductor 指揮家
snare drum 小鼓
bass drum 大鼓
drums 鼓
guitar 吉他
violin 小提琴
xylophone 木琴
maracas 沙鈴
French horn 法國號
trombone 長號
trumpet 小號

flute 長笛
clarinet 單簧管
reed organ 簧風琴

In the Library
在圖書館裡
librarian 圖書館員
circulation desk 借書處
newspaper 報紙
book 書
cover 封面
page 頁
table of contents 目次
index 索引
dictionary 字典
illustrated book 圖鑑
picture book 圖畫書
biography 傳記
magazine 雜誌
fairy tales 童話故事
comic book 漫畫書

fiction story 小說
photograph collection 寫真集
reference book 參考書
read 閱讀
borrow 借
return 歸還

其他
study 學習、研讀
think 思考
read 閱讀
write 書寫
calculate 計算
copy 抄寫、複製
ask a question 提問
answer 回答
discuss 討論
give a presentation 發表
turn in 繳交
raise my hand 舉手

16

NATURE 大自然 (1)

Animals 動物
giraffe 長頸鹿
deer 鹿
kangaroo 袋鼠
donkey 驢子
zebra 斑馬
cheetah 獵豹
leopard 豹
elephant 象
bear 熊
rhinoceros 犀牛
tiger 老虎
koala 無尾熊
squirrel 松鼠
bat 蝙蝠
panda 貓熊
lion 獅子
snake 蛇
lizard 蜥蜴
iguana 鬣蜥蜴
wolf 狼
monkey 猴子
raccoon dog 貉

camel 駱駝
fox 狐狸
raccoon 浣熊
gorilla 大猩猩
chimpanzee 黑猩猩
hippopotamus 河馬
alligator 短吻鱷
hay 乾草
bull 公牛
rat 老鼠
calf 小牛
cow 母牛
mole 鼴鼠
turkey 火雞
pasture 牧場、牧草地
duck 鴨
goose 鵝
frog 青蛙
tadpole 蝌蚪
farm 農場
crow 烏鴉
scarecrow 稻草人
sheep 綿羊

lamb 小羊、羔羊
goat 山羊
piglet 小豬
pig 豬
horse 馬
chick 小雞
hen 母雞
goldfish 金魚
parrot 鸚鵡
parakeet 長尾鸚鵡
tortoise 龜、陸龜
dog 狗
chameleon 變色龍
rabbit 兔子
guinea pig 天竺鼠
hamster 倉鼠
cat 貓
mouse 小鼠
puppy 小狗
kitten 小貓

Birds 鳥
cuckoo 布穀鳥
pigeon 鴿子
sparrow 麻雀
seagull 海鷗
eagle 老鷹
pheasant 雉雞
penguin 企鵝
pelican 鵜鶘
swan 天鵝
swallow 燕子
hawk 較小的鷹科和較
　大的隼科鳥類
nest 巢
owl 貓頭鷹
woodpecker 啄木鳥
crane 鶴
flamingo 紅鶴
peacock 孔雀
ostrich 鴕鳥
cage 籠子
bill/ beak 喙
wing 翅膀

17

NATURE 大自然 (3)

Flowers 花
cactus 仙人掌
iris 鳶尾花
sunflower 向日葵
rape blossoms 油菜花
morning glory 牽牛花
dandelion 蒲公英
cosmos 波斯菊
rose 玫瑰
carnation 康乃馨
dahlia 大理菊
violet 紫羅蘭
lily 百合
orchid 蘭花
cherry blossoms 櫻花
daffodil 水仙
tulip 鬱金香
daisy 雛菊
poppy 罌粟
lily of the valley 鈴蘭
chrysanthemum 菊花
hydrangea 繡球花

petal 花瓣
bud 花蕾、芽
leaf 葉子
thorn 刺
stem 莖
root 根
bulb 球莖
seed 種子
tree 樹
twig 細枝
branch 樹枝
trunk 樹幹
vine 藤、蔓

At the Beach
在海灘
lighthouse 燈塔
surfer 衝浪者
swim ring 游泳圈
snorkel 潛水呼吸管設備
beach umbrella（海
　灘等處）遮陽傘

sunscreen 防晒乳
sandcastle 沙堡
seashell 貝殼
sunglasses 太陽眼鏡
sand 沙
wave 海浪
horizon 水平線
rock 岩石
shore 海岸
swimmer 游泳者
seawater 海水
beach ball 海灘球
swimming trunks 泳褲
swimsuit 泳衣
shaved ice 刨冰
lifeguard 救生員
beach 海灘

In the Country
在鄉間
cliff 懸崖
stream 河流

rice field 稻田
rainbow 彩虹
volcano 火山
campsite 露營地
hammock 吊床
tent 帳篷
sleeping bag 睡袋
backpack 背包
summit 山頂
echo 回音
orchard 果園
cave 洞穴
forest 森林
valley 山谷
waterfall 瀑布
woods 樹林
mountain hut 山間小屋
field 田地
hill 小丘、丘陵
grass 草
tunnel 隧道
lake 湖泊

19

NATURE 大自然 (2)

Insects 昆蟲
web 網
beetle 甲蟲
caterpillar 毛蟲
moth 蛾
spider 蜘蛛
stag beetle 鍬形蟲
honeycomb 蜂巢
bee 蜜蜂
mosquito 蚊子
honey 蜂蜜
snail 蝸牛
ant 螞蟻
praying mantis 螳螂
butterfly 蝴蝶
dragonfly 蜻蜓
cicada 蟬
longicorn 天牛
gecko 壁虎
ladybug 瓢蟲
grasshopper 蚱蜢

firefly 螢火蟲
toad 蟾蜍
water strider 水黽
earthworm 蚯蚓
pupa 蛹
wing 翅膀
larva 幼蟲

Ocean Fish
海裡的魚
shark 鯊魚
shellfish 貝
sea otter 海獺
ray 魟魚
blowfish 河魨
sardine 沙丁魚
whale 鯨魚
sunfish 翻車魚
porgy 鯛魚
seaweed 海藻
starfish 海星

sea anemone 海葵
sea urchin 海膽
crab 蟹
sea 海洋
turtle 海龜、龜
tuna 鮪魚
dolphin 海豚
octopus 章魚
seal 海豹
sea horse 海馬
squid 烏賊、魷魚
jellyfish 水母
shrimp 蝦
flatfish 比目魚
angler 鮟鱇魚
prawn 明蝦

River Fish
河川裡的魚
scale 鱗
fin 鰭
gill 鰓
tail fin 尾鰭
carp 鯉魚
crucian carp 鯽魚
trout 鱒魚
eel 鰻魚
catfish 鯰魚
fishing 釣魚
fishing rod 釣魚竿
salmon 鮭魚
river 河流
goby 蝦虎魚
loach 泥鰍
crayfish 螯蝦、小龍蝦

NATURE 大自然 (4)

The Weather 天氣
It's sunny. 晴朗的
It's stormy. 暴風雨的
It's hot. 炎熱的
It's cloudy. 多雲的
It's humid. 潮溼的
It's cold. 寒冷的
It's rainy. 多雨的
It's foggy. 有霧的
It's warm. 溫暖的
It's snowy. 下雪的
It's windy. 風大的
It's freezing. 冰凍的
cloud 雲
rain 雨
rainbow 彩虹
snow 雪
wind 風
storm 暴風雨
typhoon 颱風
thunder 雷

Space 宇宙
rocket 火箭
astronaut 太空人
sun 太陽
Mercury 水星
Venus 金星
Earth 地球
moon 月球
Mars 火星
comet 彗星
Jupiter 木星
Saturn 土星
Uranus 天王星
Neptune 海王星
orbit 軌道
alien 外星人
shooting star 流星
North Star 北極星
constellation 星座
Big Dipper 北斗七星
Milky Way 銀河

telescope 望遠鏡
star 星星
full moon 滿月
half-moon 半月
crescent moon 眉月

其他
paw 腳掌、爪
whiskers 鬍鬚
claw 爪
tail 尾巴
bark 吠叫
groom（寵物）美容、整潔梳理
scratch 抓
Sit! 坐下！
Down! 趴下！
Beg! 拜託！
Stay! 等等！
Give me your paw! 握手！

SPORTS and AMUSMENTS
運動和娛樂 (1)

Outdoor Games
戶外遊戲

play kick-the-can 玩踢罐子
ride a unicycle 騎單輪車
play tag 玩鬼捉人
play hide-and-seek 玩躲貓貓
play dodge ball 玩躲避球
roller-skate （輪式）溜冰
play cops and robbers 玩官兵
　　捉強盜
jump rope 跳繩
ride a skateboard 溜滑板
blow bubbles 吹泡泡

Toys 玩具

stuffed animal （動物造型）
　　填充娃娃
video game 電玩遊戲
robot 機器人

toy car 玩具車
jump rope 跳繩
jack-in-the-box 玩偶盒、驚喜盒
doll 洋娃娃、玩偶
water pistol 水槍
radio-controlled car 遙控汽車
jigsaw puzzle 拼圖
kite 風箏
figurine 模型
trampoline 彈跳床
teddy bear 泰迪熊
cards 紙牌
drone 無人機
hula hoop 呼拉圈
dice 骰子
piggy bank 小豬撲滿
yo-yo 溜溜球
slime 黏土

Indoor Games
室內遊戲

play rock-paper-scissors 猜拳
paly with blocks 堆積木
do origami 摺紙
play ringtoss 玩套圈圈
paly cards 玩紙牌
do a jigsaw puzzle 拼拼圖
play bingo 玩賓果遊戲
play musical chairs 玩搶椅子
play with a yo-yo 玩溜溜球
do a crossword puzzle 做填字
　　遊戲
play with dolls 玩洋娃娃、
　　玩玩偶

SPORTS and AMUSMENTS
運動和娛樂 (3)

TV 電視

power switch 電源開關
channel selector 頻道選擇器
volume button 音量按鈕
screen 螢幕
DVD recorder DVD燒錄機
remote control 遙控
watch TV 看電視
turn on the TV 開電視
turn off the TV 關電視
TV program 電視節目
quiz show 益智節目
news program 新聞
cartoons 卡通
documentary 紀錄片
talk show 脫口秀
sportscast 體育節目
TV commercial 電視廣告

Video Games 電玩遊戲

win the game 遊戲獲勝
lose the game 遊戲落敗
game console 遊戲機
video game software 電玩遊
　　戲軟體
role-playing game 角色扮演遊戲
action game 動作遊戲
puzzle game 益智遊戲
racing game 競速遊戲
board game 圖版遊戲
shooting game 射擊遊戲

Computers 電腦

laptop 筆記型電腦
tablet computer 平板電腦
start the computer 開機
shut down the computer 關機

click 點擊
e-mail address 電子郵件地址
e-mail 電子郵件
Internet 網路
website 網站
screen 螢幕
keyboard 鍵盤
mouse 滑鼠
power switch 電源開關
search 搜尋
send an e-mail 寄送電子郵件
receive an e-mail 接收電子郵件
password 密碼
log on 登入
log off 登出
download 下載

Language Games 文字遊戲

word chain game 文字接龍遊戲
cap 棒球帽
pen 原子筆
notebook 筆記本
knife 刀子
egg 蛋
crossword puzzle 填字遊戲
down 縱向
across 橫向
tongue twister 繞口令
riddle 謎語

Fortune-telling 算命

crystal gazing 水晶球占卜

card reading 塔羅牌占卜
palm reading 看手相
blood type 血型
fortune cookie 幸運餅乾
horoscope 占星術
Capricorn 摩羯座
Aquarius 水瓶座
Pisces 雙魚座
Aries 牡羊座
Taurus 金牛座
Gemini 雙子座
Cancer 巨蟹座
Leo 獅子座
Virgo 處女座
Libra 天秤座
Scorpio 天蠍座
Sagittarius 射手座

At the Amusement Park 在遊樂園裡

go-cart 卡丁車
stage 舞臺
popcorn 爆米花
stand 攤子
merry-go-round 旋轉木馬
mascot 吉祥物
entrance 入口
roller coaster 雲霄飛車
Ferris wheel 摩天輪
line 排隊
whirling teacups 旋轉咖啡杯
maze 迷宮
parade 遊行
haunted house 鬼屋

souvenir shop 紀念品商店
clown 小丑

Trips 旅行

departure 出發
boarding 登機
arrival 抵達
stay 停留
hotel 飯店
sightseeing 觀光
shopping 購物
going home 回家
camera 相機
ticket 機票
passport 護照
money 錢
map 地圖
souvenir 紀念品

Sports 運動

soccer 足球
goal 球門、終點、得分
goalkeeper 守門員
referee 裁判
baseball 棒球
glove 手套
pitcher 投手
ball 球
bat 球棒
catcher 捕手
batter 打擊手
swimming 游泳
crawl 自由式
breaststroke 蛙式
swimming goggles 泳鏡
gymnastics 體操
(American) football（美式）足球

basketball 籃球
tennis 網球
volleyball 排球
badminton 羽球
ice hockey 冰上曲棍球
table tennis 桌球
softball 壘球
golf 高爾夫球
rugby（英式）橄欖球
boxing 拳擊
track and field 田徑
horseback riding 騎馬
ballet 芭蕾
surfing 衝浪
skiing 滑雪
ice skating 溜冰
wrestling 摔角

其他

play 進行（運動）、打或踢（球）
run 跑
throw 投、擲、拋
hit 打、擊
catch 接
kick 踢
pass 傳遞
shoot 射
dribble 運球
attack 進攻
defend 防守
swim 游

EVENTS 事件 (1)

Months 月
season 季節
spring 春
summer 夏
fall/ autumn 秋
winter 冬
January 一月
February 二月
March 三月
April 四月
May 五月
June 六月
July 七月
August 八月
September 九月
October 十月
November 十一月
December 十二月
a week 一星期
Monday 星期一
Tuesday 星期二
Wednesday 星期三
Thursday 星期四
Friday 星期五
Saturday 星期六
Sunday 星期日
weekday 平日
weekend 週末

Holidays 節日
New Year's Day 元旦
Saint Valentine('s) Day 情人節
Easter 復活節
Easter egg 復活節彩蛋
bunny 兔子
April Fool's Day 愚人節
Mother's Day 母親節
Father's Day 父親節
Halloween 萬聖夜（萬聖節前夕）
bat 蝙蝠
ghost 鬼
jack-o'-lantern 南瓜燈

Thanksgiving Day 感恩節
pumpkin pie 南瓜派
turkey 火雞
Christmas Day 聖誕節
reindeer 馴鹿
holly 冬青
wreath 花環
Santa Claus 聖誕老人
bell 鈴
light bulb 燈泡
Christmas tree 聖誕樹
ornament 裝飾品

LIFE 生活 (1)

Health 健康
I feel sick. 我覺得噁心想吐。
I have a headache. 我覺得頭痛。
I have a stomachache. 我肚子痛。
I have a sore throat. 我喉嚨痛。
I have a pain here. 我覺得這裡疼痛。
I have a cold. 我感冒了。
I have a cough. 我咳嗽。
I have diarrhea. 我腹瀉。
I feel itchy here. 我覺得這裡很癢。
I'm fine. 我很好。
I have a toothache. 我牙齒痛。
I have a fever. 我發燒了。
I broke my arm. 我的手臂骨折了。

Clothing 服裝
collar 領子
cardigan 開襟羊毛衫
shorts 短褲
dress 洋裝
sleeve 袖子
short sleeve 短袖
long sleeve 長袖
sweatshirt 長袖運動衣
jeans 牛仔褲
pajamas 睡衣
button 鈕釦
T-shirt T恤
skirt 裙子
zipper 拉鍊
shoes 鞋子
uniform 制服
vest 背心
blouse（女生的）上衣、襯衫
sweater 毛衣
coat 外套、大衣
pants 褲子
wedding dress 婚紗
jacket 夾克、短外套
suit 西裝
tights 緊身褲襪
glasses 眼鏡

hat 帽子
gloves 手套
socks 襪子
handkerchief 手帕
scarf 圍巾
boots 靴子
mittens 連指手套
slippers 拖鞋
suspenders 吊帶
tie 領帶
high heels 高跟鞋
scarf 領巾
cap 便帽、棒球帽
bag 袋子、包包
raincoat 雨衣
belt 腰帶
ribbon 緞帶
wallet 錢包
sneakers 球鞋
umbrella 雨傘

EVENTS 事件 (2)

School Events 學校行事

entrance ceremony 入學儀式
field trip 遠足、校外教學
field day 運動會、校外教學日
parents' day 家長日
school trip 校外教學
school festival 校慶
spring vacation 春假
summer vacation 暑假
winter vacation 寒假
graduation 畢業、畢業典禮

Parties 派對

birthday party 生日派對
streamer 飄帶、橫幅
balloon 氣球
feast 宴會
invitation card 邀請函
birthday card 生日卡片
candle 蠟燭
cake 蛋糕
present 禮物

其他

New Year's Day 元旦
Chinese New Year 農曆新年
Lantern Festival 元宵節
Children's Day 兒童節
Tomb Sweeping Day 清明節
Dragon Boat Festival 端午節
Ghost Festival 中元節
Moon Festival（Mid-Autumn
　　Festival）中秋節
Teachers' Day 教師節
Double Tenth Day 雙十節
Constitution Day 行憲紀念日
Winter Solstice 冬至

LIFE 生活 (2)

Jewelry and Cosmetics 珠寶和化妝品

pierced earring 穿耳式耳環
hair spray 髮膠
lipstick 口紅
nail polish 指甲油
powder（化妝用）粉
cosmetics 化妝品
bracelet 手鐲
hairpin 髮夾
earring 耳環
jewel 寶石
diamond 鑽石
ruby 紅寶石
hair tie 髮圈
ring 戒指
comb 梳子
perfume 香水
nail clippers 指甲剪

Jobs 工作

painter 畫家
politician 政治家
hairdresser 美髮師
actor 演員
cook/ chef 廚師
singer 歌手
fashion designer 時裝設計師
flight attendant 空服員
pilot 飛行員
comedian 喜劇演員
model 模特兒
photographer 攝影師
lawyer 律師
cartoonist 漫畫家
pianist 鋼琴家
computer programmer 電腦
　程式設計師
tennis player 網球選手
bus driver 公車司機

announcer 播音員
carpenter 木匠
tour guide 導遊
public official 公職人員
teacher 教師
nursery school teacher 托兒所
　或幼兒園老師
police officer 警察
judge 法官
voice actor 配音員
scientist 科學家
doctor 醫師
nurse 護理師
florist 花匠
farmer 農夫
office worker 上班族
astronaut 太空人
firefighter 消防員
vet 獸醫

LIFE 生活 (3)

The World 世界
the world map 世界地圖
north 北
west 西
south 南
east 東
the U.K. 英國
Europe 歐洲
France 法國
Germany 德國
Spain 西班牙
Italy 義大利
Egypt 埃及
the Atlantic Ocean 大西洋
Africa 非洲
Russia 俄羅斯
South Korea 南韓
Asia 亞洲
China 中國
India 印度
Thailand 泰國

Singapore 新加坡
Japan 日本
the Pacific Ocean 太平洋
Australia 澳大利亞
Oceania 大洋洲
New Zealand 紐西蘭
Canada 加拿大
North America 北美洲
the U.S.A. (America) 美國
Mexico 墨西哥
Brazil 巴西
South America 南美洲

Telephone 電話
app 行動軟體應用程式
smartphone 智慧型手機
telephone 電話
charger 充電器
cellphone 手機
text message 簡訊
emoticon 表情符號

其他
Northern hemisphere 北半球
Southern hemisphere 南半球
equator 赤道
North Pole 北極
South Pole 南極
line of longitude 經線
line of latitude 緯線

COLORS, SHAPES and NUMBERS
顏色、形狀和數字 (2)

Numbers 數字
zero 0
one 1
two 2
three 3
four 4
five 5
six 6
seven 7
eight 8
nine 9
ten 10
eleven 11
twelve 12
thirteen 13
fourteen 14
fifteen 15
sixteen 16
seventeen 17

eighteen 18
nineteen 19
twenty 20
thirty 30
forty 40
fifty 50
sixty 60
seventy 70
eighty 80
ninety 90
one hundred 100
one thousand 1000
ten thousand 1萬
one hundred thousand 10萬
one million 100萬
one hundred million 1億
one billion 10億
first 第一
second 第二

third 第三
fourth 第四
fifth 第五
twenty-first 第二十一
hundredth 第一百
once 一次
twice 兩次
three times 三次
four times 四次
whole 1（全部）
a half 1/2
a quarter 1/4
a third 1/3
three quarters 3/4
two thirds 2/3

Colors 顏色
deep green 深綠色
green 綠色
yellow green 黃綠色
light blue 淺藍色
blue 藍色
ultramarine 深藍色
purple 紫色
magenta 紫紅色
red 紅色
vermilion 朱紅色
orange 橙色
yellow 黃色
pink 粉紅色
white 白色
gray 灰色
brown 棕色、褐色
black 黑色
gold 金色
silver 銀色

Shapes 形狀
triangle 三角形
diamond 菱形
prism 角柱體
cube 立方體
cylinder 圓柱體
pyramid 角錐體
arrow 箭頭
whirl 螺旋形
sphere 球體
circle 圓形
cone 圓錐體
square 正方形
heart 心形
rectangle 長方形
line 線
point 點
angle 角、角度
diameter 直徑

center 中心
radius 半徑

Quantities 數量
a slice of bread 一片麵包
a can of soda 一罐汽水
a bar of chocolate 一條巧克力
a bottle of water 一瓶水
a box of matches 一盒火柴
a sheet of paper 一張紙
a jar of jam 一瓶果醬
a bag of chips 一包洋芋片
a piece of cake 一塊蛋糕
a cup of coffee 一杯咖啡
a pair of pants 一條褲子
a carton of milk 一盒牛奶
a roll of toilet paper 一卷衛生紙
a glass of milk 一杯牛奶
a pair of shoes 一雙鞋

30

Units 單位
millimeter 毫米/公釐
centimeter 釐米/公分
meter 米/公尺
kilometer 千米/公里
weight 重量
gram 公克
kilogram 公斤
ton 公噸
capacity 容量
milliliter 毫升
deciliter 分升/公合
liter 公升
degree 度
temperature 溫度
angle 角度、角

Time 時間
clock 時鐘
wristwatch 手錶

one-oh-five 01:05
one ten 01:10
one fifteen 01:15
one thirty 01:30
one forty-five 01:45
one fifty-five 01:55
one second 1秒鐘
one minute 1分鐘
one hour 1小時
one day 1天
one week 1星期
one month 1個月
one year 1年
one century 1世紀
morning 早上
afternoon 下午
evening 傍晚
night 晚上

其他
yesterday 昨天
this morning 今天早上
today 今天
tonight 今晚
tomorrow 明天
last week 上個星期
this week 這個星期
next week 下個星期
now 現在
before lunch 午餐前
after lunch 午餐後
ten years ago 10年前

32